Charles Kendall Adams

Christopher Columbus

His Life and Works

Charles Kendall Adams

Christopher Columbus
His Life and Works

ISBN/EAN: 9783337027742

Printed in Europe, USA, Canada, Australia, Japan

Cover: Foto ©Raphael Reischuk / pixelio.de

More available books at **www.hansebooks.com**

THE LOTTO PORTRAIT OF COLUMBUS.

"MAKERS OF AMERICA"

CHRISTOPHER COLUMBUS

His Life and His Work

BY

CHARLES KENDALL ADAMS, LL.D.

PRESIDENT OF CORNELL UNIVERSITY

NEW YORK

DODD, MEAD AND COMPANY

1892

𝔘𝔫𝔦𝔳𝔢𝔯𝔰𝔦𝔱𝔶 𝔓𝔯𝔢𝔰𝔰:

John Wilson and Son, Cambridge.

TO

J. J. HAGERMAN,

Nobleman and Friend,

THIS VOLUME IS AFFECTIONATELY DEDICATED

BY THE AUTHOR.

PREFACE.

In this little volume I have made an attempt to present in popular form the results of the latest researches in regard to the life and work of Columbus.

While constant use has been made of the original authorities, it has been my effort to interpret the conflicting statements with which these sources abound, in the spirit of modern criticism. The principal authorities used have been the Letters and the Journal of Columbus, the History of the Admiral purporting to be by his son Fernando, the histories of the time by Las Casas, Bernaldez, Oviedo, Peter Martyr, and Herrera, and the invaluable collection of documents by Navarrete. Of the greatest importance are the writings of Columbus and Las Casas.

As will appear in the course of the volume, the writings of the Admiral abound in passages that are contradictory or irreconcilable. In the interpretation of conflicting statements, assistance has been received from the numerous writings of Henry Harrisse. The researches of this acute critic in the manuscript records, as well as in the published writings of Italy and Spain, make his works indispensable to a correct understanding of the age of Columbus.

I have not, however, been able to adopt without reservation his views in regard to the work attributed to the son of the Admiral. The force of Harrisse's reasoning is unquestionable ; but, as it seems to me, there is internal evidence that the author of the book, whether Fernando or not, had unusual opportunities for knowledge in regard to the matters about which he wrote. While, therefore, I have used the work with great caution, I have not felt justified in rejecting it as altogether spurious.

The reader will not go far in the perusal of this volume without perceiving that I have endeavoured to emancipate myself from the thraldom of that uncritical admiration in which it has been fashionable to hold the Discoverer, ever since Washington Irving threw over the subject the romantic and bewitching charm of his literary skill. Irving revealed the spirit with which he wrote when he decried what he was pleased to call " that pernicious erudition which busies itself with undermining the pedestals of our national monuments." Irving's was not the spirit of modern scholarship. We should seek the truth at whatever hazard. While directed by this motive in the course of all my investigations into the life and work of Columbus, I have tried, on the one hand, to avoid the common error of bringing him to the bar of the present age for trial, and, on the other, not to shrink from judging him in accordance with those canons of justice which are applicable alike to all time.

C. K. A.

CORNELL UNIVERSITY,
     March 10, 1892.

TABLE OF CONTENTS.

————◆————

CHRISTOPHER COLUMBUS.

CHAPTER I.

EARLY YEARS.

AT the northwest corner of the Italian peninsula the coast-line, as it approaches the French border, bends around to the west in such a way as to form a kind of rounded angle, which, according to the fertile fancy of the Greeks, resembles the human knee. It was probably in recognition of this geographical peculiarity that the hamlet established at this point received some centuries before the Christian era the name which has since been evolved into Genoa. The situation is not only one of the most picturesque in Europe, but it is peculiarly adapted to the development of a small maritime city. For many miles it is the only point at which Nature has afforded a good opportunity for a harbor. Its geographical relations with the region of the Alps and the plains of northern Italy seem to have designated it as the natural point where a common desire for gain should bring into profitable relations the trading propensities of the people along the shores of the Mediterranean. During nearly two thousand years the situation was

made all the more favourable by the ease with which
it might be defended; for the range of mountains,
which encircles it at a distance of only a few miles,
made it easy for the inhabitants to protect themselves
against the assaults of their enemies.

The favouring conditions thus afforded gave to
Genoa early in the Christian era a commercial pres-
tige of some importance. The turbulence of the
Middle Ages made rapidity of growth quite impossible; but in the time of the Crusades this picturesque city received a large share of that impulse which
gave so much life to Venice and the other maritime
towns of Italy. Like other cities of its kind, it was
filled with seafaring men. It is easy to believe that
the boys who grew up in Genoa during the centuries
of the Crusades and immediately after, had their imaginations and memories filled to overflowing with
accounts of such wonderful adventures as those which,
about that time, found expression in the writings of
Marco Polo and John de Mandeville. The tales of
seafaring adventurers always have a wonderful attrac-
tion for boys; and we can well imagine that the yarns
spun by the returning sailors of the fourteenth and
fifteenth centuries had an altogether peculiar and
exceptional fascination.

It was probably in this city of Genoa that Christopher Columbus was born. It is certain that his
parents lived there at the middle of the fifteenth century. Whether his father had been in Genoa very
many years is doubtful; for there is one bit of record
that seems to indicate his moving into the city at

some time between 1448 and 1451. That the ances-
tors of the family had lived in that vicinity ever since
the twelfth or thirteenth century may be regarded as
certain. But beyond this fact very little rests upon
strict historical evidence. This uncertainty, springing
as it does from the fact that the name Columbus appears very often in the records of northern Italy during the century before the birth of Christopher, has
brought into controversy a multitude of importunate
claimants. If a kind of selfish pride was indicated
by the fact that —

> " Seven cities claimed the Homer dead,
>   In which the living Homer begged his bread," —

the same characteristic of human nature was shown in
northern Italy in more than two-fold measure ; for no
less than sixteen Italian towns have tried to lift themselves into greater importance by setting up a claim
to the distinction of having been the birthplace of the
Great Discoverer. But these several claims have not
succeeded in producing any conclusive evidence. The
question is still in some doubt. At least twice in his
writings Columbus speaks of himself as having been
born at Genoa ; and he was generally recognized as
a Genoese by his contemporaries. But his parents
seem to have been somewhat migratory in their
habits. The records show that the father of Christopher was the owner of some property in several of
the towns along the foot of the Alps. Besides his
other estates, which for the most part came from his
wife, he had a house in one of the suburbs of the city

of Genoa, and also one in the city itself. Within a
few years the Marquis Marcello Staglieno, a learned
Genoese antiquary, has established the fact that No.
37 Vico Dritto Ponticello in Genoa was owned by
Dominico Columbus, the father of Christopher, during
the early years of Christopher's life. But it has not
yet been shown by any documentary evidence that he
ever lived there. The ownership of this house, and
of one in the suburbs, establishes a very strong probability that in one of them Christopher Columbus was
born. It cannot be said, however, that the exact
spot has been determined with certainty; and in view
of the conflicting evidence, Genoa is to be regarded
as the place of his birth only in that broad sense
which would include a considerable number of the
surrounding dependencies. Bernaldez, Peter Martyr,
Oviedo, and Las Casas speak of his birthplace as
being, not the city, but the province of Genoa.

The original authorities, moreover, are as conflicting in regard to time as in regard to place. The
most definite statement we have is that of Bernaldez,
the contemporary and friend as well as the historian
of the discoverer. Columbus at one time was an in-
mate of the house of Bernaldez, and hence it would
seem that the historian had good opportunities for
ascertaining the truth. But the information he gives
in regard to the date of Columbus's birth is only
inferential, and is far from satisfactory. He says
that the Admiral died in 1506, " at the age of seventy, a little more or a little less." This is the statement which has led Humboldt, Navarrete, and Irving,

as well as other careful writers, to believe that the
date of his birth should be fixed at 1436. But the
acceptance of this date is involved in serious difficulties. The discoverer, it is true, nowhere tells us his
exact age ; but frequently in his writings he not only
mentions the number of years he had followed the
sea, but he says he began his nautical career at the
age of fourteen. These several statements, put together,
point very definitely and consistently to a date nearly
or quite ten years later than that indicated by Bernaldez. It cannot be claimed that the statements of
Columbus are so exact as to be absolutely free from
doubt ; but in the absence of any record of his birth,
they are at least entitled to careful consideration. In
a letter written in 1503 the Admiral says that he was
thirty-eight when he entered the service of Spain. As
he first went to Spain in 1484 or 1485, we are obliged
to infer that the service he referred to began either in
that year or at a later period. This would indicate
that he was born in 1446 or later. In 1501, moreover, he wrote that it was forty years since at the age
of fourteen he entered upon a seafaring life. This,
too, would point to about 1447 as the date of his
birth. These, and other statements of a similar nature, are at least enough to justify the inquiry whether
the error is probably with Columbus or with Bernaldez. In the case of the historian, the very phrase
" seventy, a little more or a little less," carries with it
an implication of uncertainty. It seemed to imply
that the author judged of the age of Columbus simply
from his appearance. Now, there is abundant evi-

dence that the superabounding anxieties and perplexities of his career had the natural effect of making him prematurely old. We have the statement of his son that his hair was gray at the age of thirty; and it is easy to believe that the perplexing vicissitudes of his career deepened and intensified the evidences of age with unnatural rapidity. If, as we have so often and so justly heard, it is anxiety and perplexity that bring on premature age and decay, surely Columbus of all men must have been old long before he reached the goal of threescore and ten. In view of all these facts, it is probable that the conjecture of Bernaldez was incorrect, though very naturally so, and that the date indicated by the figures of Columbus himself is the one that is entitled to most credence. But all we can say on the subject is that Christopher Columbus was probably born in or about the year 1446. Harrisse, who has scrutinized all the evidence with characteristic acumen, has reached the conclusion that Columbus was born between the 25th of March, 1446, and the 20th of March, 1447.

He was the eldest son of Dominico Columbus and Susannah Fontanarossa, his wife. The other children were Bartholomew and Giacomo, or, as the Spanish call it, Diego, and a sister, of whom nothing of importance is known. The kith and kin of the family for some generations devoted themselves to the humble vocation of wool-combers. The property of the family, of which at the time Columbus was born there was barely enough for a modest competency, appears to have come chiefly from the mother.

That the father was a man of exceptional energy, is evinced by the vigour with which he undertook and carried on the various enterprises with which he was connected. In his business, however, he was only moderately prosperous; and so the family was obliged to content itself with a small income.

The early life of Columbus is still quite thickly enshrouded with uncertainty. His education included a reading knowledge of Latin, but his training could have been neither comprehensive nor thorough. Many of the historians, resting upon the statement of Fernando Columbus, assert that he spent a year in the study of cosmogony at the University of Pavia. But the statement is inherently improbable, and rests upon evidence that is altogether inadequate. His father was not in condition to send him to the university without inconvenience. It was the custom of those times for the son to be trained for the vocation of the father. Such a training the young Christopher had, and a formal knowledge of geography, or cosmogony, as the study was then more generally called, would not have added much to his chances of business success. If he went to the university at all, he must have concluded his studies before he was fourteen. Pavia at the time afforded no special advantages for the prosecution of this study, — indeed, it cannot now be discovered that it possessed any advantages whatever. On the contrary, that celebrated university was devoted with singular exclusiveness to the teaching of philosophy, law, and medicine. There is no evidence in the

records of the university that Columbus was ever
there. The explorer himself, though he often refers
to his early studies, nowhere intimates that he was
ever at the university. It was not till more than
fifty years after the death of Columbus that his son
made the statement on which all subsequent assertions on the subject rest for authority. That the
explorer was ever at the university is overwhelmingly
improbable.

We know, however, from the best of evidence that
he early became interested in geographical studies.
His father's business does not seem to have been
very prosperous, — at least, we find him about this
time selling out his little property in Genoa and
establishing himself at Savona. Meantime, the youthful Christopher found himself yielding to the strong
current which in those years carried so many of the
Genoese into a life of maritime adventure. If our
conjecture in regard to the time of his birth is correct, it was about 1460 when he took his first voyage.
From that initiative experience for about ten years,
that is to say until 1470, we have only glimpses here
and there of the events of his life. Nor can we
regard the details of this experience as important,
except as they throw light upon the development of
his intelligence and character. Fortunately for this
purpose evidence is not altogether wanting. Bits
of information have been picked up here and there,
which, though it is impossible to weave them very
confidently into a connected whole, still show, in a
general way, the nature of the training he received

during those important years. If we condense into a
useful form all that is positively known of his life
during the ten years from the time he was fourteen
until he was twenty-four, we shall perhaps conclude
that there are only three results that are worthy of
note.

The first is the fact that he had considerable maritime experience of a very turbulent nature. There
is some reason to believe that he accompanied the
unsuccessful expedition of John of Anjou against
Naples in 1459. However this may have been, it is
certain that he joined several of the expeditions of
the celebrated corsairs bearing the same family name
of Columbus. Modern eulogists of the great discoverer have hesitated to write the ugly word which
indicates the nature of the business in which these
much-dreaded fleets were engaged; but the state
papers of the time uniformly refer to the elder of
these commanders as "the Pirate Columbus." To
the younger they also refer in no more complimentary
terms. Fernando Columbus is authority for the statement that his father accompanied the celebrated expedition that fought the great battle off Cape St.
Vincent. But the statement is a curious illustration
of the necessity of accepting the assurances of this
historian with extreme caution. He says that it was
by escaping from the wreck of the fleet that his
father came for the first time to his new home in
Portugal. Now, we know that the battle alluded to
did not take place until 1485, the year after Columbus left Portugal and went to Spain; and as he was

otherwise occupied ever after he reached Spanish soil, it is not possible that the young navigator was even with the fleet during the engagement. We know, moreover, that he moved to Lisbon before 1473.

But the evidence is conclusive that the Admiral had accompanied the piratical fleets on several former expeditions. The records of Venice show that a decree was passed against the elder pirate Columbus, July 20, 1469, and another against the younger on the 17th of March, 1470. Although these fulminations did not put an end to this peculiar warfare, they are of interest in this connnection as showing the school in which Columbus received a considerable part of his early nautical training and experience.

There may be some doubt as to how much importance should be attached to the circumstantial statement of Fernando in regard to his father's connection with these celebrated freebooters. The narrative certainly contains some irreconcilable contradictions; but although Fernando may have been mistaken in the details, he can hardly have been mistaken in the fact that his father accompanied several of these expeditions. A matter of that kind could hardly fail to have been talked about in the presence of the children. The boys may have received erroneous impressions in reference to details. As time went on, it was naturally easy for events with which the father was definitely connected to become confused with those with which he had nothing whatever to do. But the great fact of his connection with the fleet, of his experience on the piratical ships, can hardly have been an invention of the son. There were two pirates by the name of Columbus, — the younger being, according to one authority, the son, according to another, the nephew of the elder. Fernando gives us to understand distinctly that his father was engaged in the service of both. He moreover considers this so much a matter of pride that he endeavours to establish the fact of a relationship between the two families. The nature of the school in which the young Columbus received a part of his training may be inferred by the fact that the younger of the corsairs in the course of a few years captured as many as eighty fleets, — a part of them in the Mediterranean, and a part in the open sea. During a large portion of the latter half of the fifteenth century, these daring corsairs were the dread of every fleet against whom they were employed.

There is also evidence of another schooling of a somewhat similar nature. During the fifteenth century the Portuguese were engaged in the slave-trade on the coast of Africa; and we are told that Columbus sailed several times with them to the coast of Guinea as if he had been one of them.

It must have been during this period also that the events occurred which Columbus described in a letter written to one of the Spanish monarchs in 1495. He says, —

"King René (whom God has taken to himself) sent me to Tunis to capture the galley 'Fernandina.' Arriving at the island of San Pedro in Sardinia, I learned that there were two ships and a caracca with the galley, which so

alarmed the crew that they resolved to proceed no farther, but to go to Marseilles for another vessel and a
larger crew. Upon which, being unable to force their
inclinations, I apparently yielded to their wish, and, having first changed the points of the compass, spread all
sail (for it was evening), and at daybreak we were within
the cape of Carthagena, when all believed for a certainty
that we were nearing Marseilles."

This incident shows that the schooling had given
him a full competency of intrepidity. It also shows
that the ethics of the school had had the natural
effect of relieving him of all unnecessary scruples of
conscience.

Another voyage of a very different nature was
probably made at a little later period. Unfortunately we are indebted for our knowledge of it entirely to Fernando. This is the celebrated voyage to
the north, of which so much has been made in setting up the claim that Columbus was indebted for his
idea of America to information obtained in Iceland.
It would be a great satisfaction to know just what
occurred in the course of that voyage ; but this now
seems impossible. The only record we have of the
event is that contained in a letter of Columbus quoted
by Fernando. The letter is not now known to be in
existence ; but the event alluded to seems to have
taken place in the year 1477, about four or five years
after Columbus went to Lisbon, and seven years before
he went to Spain.

Columbus is quoted as saying that he "sailed one
hundred leagues beyond the island of Tile, the south

part of which was distant from the equinoctial line seventy-three leagues, and not sixty-three, as some have asserted ; neither does it lie within the line which includes the west of that referred to by Ptolemy, but is much more westerly. To this island, which is as large as England, the English, especially from Bristol, came with their merchandise. At the time he was there, the sea was not frozen, but the tides were so great as to rise and fall twenty-six fathoms."

Nothing more is known of this voyage than is contained in this letter ; but notwithstanding the gross inaccuracies of the statement, it seems sufficient ground for believing that Columbus visited Iceland, or at least went beyond it. The size of the island indicates that it could have been no other. Whether he landed there, and if so, whether he obtained from the natives any knowledge of the continent lying far to the west and southwest, must, perhaps, forever be a matter of mere conjecture. It is, however, hardly probable that in the year 1477 Columbus would go to Iceland without making inquiries in regard to lands lying beyond. The Icelanders had long been the great explorers of the north. As we shall presently see, Columbus had already received the famous letter of Toscanelli, in which the practicability of reaching Asia by sailing due west was fully set forth ; and we know in other ways that the mind of Columbus was already fully imbued with the idea of the westward voyage of discovery. It is certain, moreover, that the Icelanders could have given him considerable valuable

information. The voyages that had been made by the
Norwegians from time to time during the eleventh
and twelfth centuries must have been known at least
by the more intelligent of the people of Iceland.   It
seems highly improbable, moreover, that Columbus,
already thirsting for more geographical knowledge,
would visit such an island without availing himself of
every opportunity of securing further information.

But on the other hand, we must not exaggerate the
importance of this conjecture.   There is no evidence
whatever that he even landed.   In all of the writings
of Columbus there is nowhere any hint of any knowledge gained from these sources ; and this very important truth should not be lost sight of in the
weighing of probabilities.   In view of all the facts, it
seems hardly possible that Columbus can have gained
from this expedition anything more than at best a
somewhat vague confirmation of the ideas and purposes that had already taken definite shape in his
mind.

Another fact worthy of note during these earlier
years was his vocation during the intervals between
his voyages.   He seems to have interlarded his more
or less piratical expeditions on the sea with the gentle experiences of a bookseller and map-maker on the
land.   The art of printing had but recently been
invented, and few books had been issued from the
press ; but there was some trade in books for all that.
There is abundant evidence that this youthful enthusiast, at the period of his life between fifteen and
twenty-four, availed himself of whatever knowledge

came in his way in regard to the subject that was beginning to fill and monopolize his mind. During the fifteenth century, as hereafter we shall have occasion to see, a large number of books on geography became generally known. Many of the classics, after lying dormant for a thousand years, sprang suddenly into life; and it is quite within the scope of a reasonable historical imagination to conjecture that, even during his years at Genoa, many of the leisure hours of what could hardly have been a very absorbing vocation as a bookseller were spent in gaining such knowledge as was possible concerning the shape and size of the earth. It would be out of place in this connection to consider details; it is enough to know that even in his earliest writings on the subject, he alluded freely to the geographical writers whose works he had read.

At some time between 1470 and 1473, Columbus changed his abode from Genoa to Lisbon. There were two facts that made this transfer of his activities both natural and beneficial. The first was that during the early part of the fifteenth century Portugal had placed herself far in advance of other nations, by her maritime expeditions and achievements. Prince Henry, with a courage and enterprise that have secured for him imperishable renown, had pushed out the boundaries of geographical knowledge, and had awakened an enthusiastic zeal for further discoveries. The fleets of Portugal had made themselves at length familiar with the west coast of Africa; and the bugbear of a tropical sea whose slimy depths were sup-

posed to make navigation impossible, had been
dispelled. The interest of every geographical explorer had been aroused and excited. Lisbon was
the centre of this new ferment.

The second consideration of importance was the
fact that Bartholomew, a younger brother of Columbus, had established himself at the Portuguese capital
as a maker and publisher of maps and charts. For
the products of this handicraft there had been created
an active demand. Nothing was more natural, then,
than that this young enthusiast, in whom there were
already welling up all kinds of maritime ambitions,
should remove to that centre of geographical knowledge and interest, and ally himself with his brother
in so congenial and promising a vocation.

It was during the years between 1473 and 1484
that a large part of the maritime experiences of
Columbus already adverted to took place. The most
of them, perhaps all of them, occurred after Columbus established himself at Lisbon. But unfortunately,
there is no contemporaneous evidence to show the
course of his life. In the records of the time we
find his name here and there in connection with such
events as those we have already mentioned ; but, as
yet, it is impossible to weave these scattered statements into a connected narrative that will bear the
test of critical examination. We are obliged, therefore, to be content with mere glimpses of individual
events and experiences.

If we have judged correctly as to the year of the
Admiral's birth, he was about twenty-six or seven

when he took up his abode in Lisbon. Not long
after this change of residence, but in what year we
cannot ascertain, an event took place which must
have had an important influence, not only on his
private life, but also on the development of his maritime plans. It was at about this time that he was
married; but when, under what circumstances, and
with whom, are questions which, notwithstanding all
that has been written on the subject, cannot now be
confidently determined. Following the statement of
Fernando, it has been customary for historians to say
that Columbus married the daughter of an old navigator of Porto Santo, Perestrello by name, to whom
Prince Henry had given the governorship of the
island in recognition of explorations and discoveries
on the coast of Africa. But like so many other of
the statements of Fernando, this turns out on examination to be extremely improbable. Harrisse is entitled to the credit of having traced the history of the
Perestrello family, and of having found the names of
the daughters, and even of their husbands. Not only
is the name Columbus lacking in these lists, but it
contains no one of the three sisters of Columbus's
wife. This, it is true, is negative evidence only, but
it is quite enough to shake our confidence in the
statement of Fernando. Of positive evidence there
is none whatever. The first mention of his having
been married at all occurs in a letter presently to be
quoted; and the second was in the clause of his will
providing for the saying of masses for his soul and for
the souls of his father, mother, and wife. This docu-

ment bears date of Aug. 25, 1505, and contains no
mention of his wife's name. A name first appears
eighteen years later, in the will of Diego, who calls
himself the son of Christopher Columbus and his wife
Donna Philippa Moñiz. Elsewhere in the same will
he refers to himself as the son of Felipa Muñiz, the
wife of Columbus, whose ashes repose in the monastery of Carmen at Lisbon. It is possible that Moñiz,
or Muñiz, was not the father's name; but the giving
of the maiden name alone in such a connection was
not usual at that time, and therefore, in the absence
of other evidence, it would seem improbable that the
name given was the surname of the father. It was
not until nearly fifty years later that the narrative
of Fernando first mentions the name of Perestrello.
Las Casas and other later writers have done nothing
but copy the statement of Fernando, without further
investigation. The matter would be of trifling significance but for the fact that later historians
have magnified this supposed marriage into a matter of considerable professional importance. Las
Casas tells us that he had learned from Diego
Columbus that the Admiral and his wife lived for
some time with the widow of Perestrello at Porto
Santo, and that " all the papers, charts, journals, and
maritime instruments " of the old navigators were
placed at his disposal. But all the evidence of this
fact now obtainable consists simply of repetitions of
this statement. The most careful search of all the
records has failed to discover a scrap of testimony that
Columbus ever lived at Porto Santo or on any of

the other islands off the coast of Africa. Harrisse has devoted more than thirty octavo pages to a very critical examination of all the evidence on the marriage of Columbus; but he is unable to reach any other positive conclusion than that very many of the early statements in regard to the matter cannot possibly be correct. As the result of his investigations, he inclines to the belief that the story of the Admiral's living at Porto Santo and profiting by the maritime possessions and experiences of Perestrello must be abandoned. Beyond the fact that the Admiral's wife bore the name of Philippa Moñiz, nothing on the subject can be regarded as absolutely known. It seems probable that Columbus was not married till after 1474; but the exact date cannot be established.

As we shall not have occasion to refer to Columbus's married life again, one fact more should here be noted. Fernando asserts that his father left Portugal in 1484 on account of the grief he experienced at the death of his wife. That the statement was incorrect, is shown by a letter, still in existence, in the handwriting of the Admiral himself. This letter, which was written to Donna Juanna de la Torre, a noble lady at the Spanish court, for the purpose of presenting his cause and arguing it with the evident expectation that his plea would reach the attention of the sovereigns, finally uses these words: —

"I beg you to take into consideration all I have written, and how I came from afar to serve these princes, — *abandoning wife and children, whom for this reason I never afterward saw.*"

This lamentable recital, written sixteen years after Columbus left Portugal for Spain, and at least nine years after he presented himself with his son Diego at La Rabida, leaves upon our minds the inevitable inference that when he fled from Portugal in 1484, he left behind him a wife and at least two children. Of his legitimate offspring, his heir and successor Diego is the only one of whom any record has been preserved. As we shall hereafter have occasion to note, Columbus left Portugal, not only in poverty, but under circumstances which made it imprudent for him to return. We are obliged to infer that his wife and children were left in indigence. Neither in the numerous writings of Columbus nor in any of the records of the time is there any allusion to the death of the wife or of the children. No letter that passed between husband and wife has ever been found. It remains only to add, on the subject of his conjugal life, that Fernando, the historian, was the natural son of Columbus by a Spanish woman, Beatriz Enriquez by name, and was born on the 15th of August, 1488.

Of the current life of Columbus at Lisbon we know very little. He seems to have been a skilful draughtsman and map-maker,—at least, in one of his letters to the Spanish king he says that God had endowed him with " ingenuity and manual skill in designing spheres and inscribing upon them in the proper places cities, rivers and mountains, isles and ports." Las Casas and Lopez de Gomera both assure us that Columbus made use of his skill as a means of livelihood.

There is also evidence that he was engaged to some extent in commercial enterprise or speculation. In his will he ordered considerable sums paid to the heirs of certain noble and rich Genoese established in Lisbon in 1482, — giving specific direction that they should not be informed from whom the money came. We know that he left Portugal secretly, and that the king, when inviting him to return, assured him immunity from civil and criminal prosecution. It has been plausibly conjectured that in the course of his commercial transactions he had incurred debts to his rich countrymen which he had never paid, and that at the last moment his conscience demanded absolution from these obligations.

Though the occasion of such debts is purely hypothetical, it is not difficult to conjecture how they may have occurred. In the fifteenth century the commercial enterprise and opportunities of Lisbon attracted thither a large number of wealthy Florentine and Genoese merchants. We are informed that they were engaged in various commercial ventures; and nothing could be more natural than that they should be ready to avail themselves of the maritime skill of their young countryman. In the journal of Columbus, under the date of Dec. 21, 1492, he wrote : —

"I have navigated the sea during twenty-three years, without noteworthy interruption; I have seen all the Levant and the Ponent; what is called the Northern Way, — that is England; and I have sailed to Guinea."

As there is no other evidence that he went to England, it is probable that the allusion here is to that northern voyage, which, as we have already seen, had had the seas about Iceland as its destination. Though it is not easy to conjecture how the phrase, "twenty-three years without noteworthy interruption," is to be reconciled with what we elsewhere learn of the years just before 1492, yet it is not difficult to understand how all the voyages referred to may have been made during that period. Before the discovery of the Cape of Good Hope by Bartholomew Diaz in December of 1487, the remotest navigable sea was not far away. To visit the North, the West, or the South was not an enterprise of long duration; and the mariner who had explored the Black Sea, the Mediterranean, the Atlantic from the equator to Iceland and the Baltic, might well claim to be familiar with all the seas that were navigable to a European.

Such were the most important of the experiences, which, so far as we can now know, gave form and fibre to the character of Columbus. If the years were full of turbulent experiences, it is evident that they were also years full of absorbing thought.

Soon after Columbus reached Lisbon, even if not before, he became possessed with the great idea that important discoveries could be made by sailing due west. Was the idea original with him? Was such a notion entertained by others? These questions, on which so much of the credit of Columbus depends, can only be answered after we take at least a brief survey of the geographical knowledge of the time.

It will perhaps never be known who first propounded the theory of the sphericity of the earth; but we are certain that it was systematically taught by the Pythagoreans of southern Italy in the sixth century before Christ. With the writings of Pythagoras, Plato was familiar, and perhaps it was from this bold western speculator that the great Athenian philosopher received the impression that finally ripened into an unquestioning belief. Pythagoras believed the earth to be a sphere, and his views and theories are set forth in two of Plato's works.

But it was the great successor of Plato who was to have the credit of giving these views systematic form. In a treatise "On the Heavens" Aristotle gave a formal summary of the grounds leading to a belief in the earth's sphericity.

Greece bequeathed this doctrine to Rome, where it was specifically taught by Pliny and Hyginus, and was referred to with seeming approval by Cicero and Ovid. From the literature of Rome it passed into many of the school-books of the Middle Ages.

The Greeks and Romans were fertile as speculators, but as navigators they really did very little. Not until the last days of the Republic did the existence of lands beyond the sea become generally known. It was in the time of Sulla that Sertorius brought back the curious story that, when on an expedition to Bætica, he fell in with certain sailors, who declared that they had just returned from the Atlantic islands, which they described as distant ten thousand stadia, or about twelve hundred and fifty miles, from Africa, and as having a wonderful flora and a still more wonderful climate. It was not until a few years later that the Canaries became known as the Fortunate Islands.

Notwithstanding all that had been done by the Tyrians and Carthaginians, Pliny refers to the Pillars of Hercules as the limit of navigation.

No systematic effort to extend the boundaries of geographical knowledge can be attributed to the Romans. There was no international competition in trade, for the reason that Rome had come to be self-reliant, and, in theory at least, to possess everything that was of value. Interest therefore was purely speculative. There was no compass; there were none but small ships.

Added to this, it must be said that there was a general and vivid horror of the western ocean. Pindar declared that no one, however brave, could pass beyond Gades; "for only a god," he said, "might voyage in those waters."

The views of the Romans were set forth in somewhat systematic form by Strabo and Pomponius Mela. The work of Mela, written during the first half of the first century, had considerable influence throughout the Middle Ages. The first edition was printed in 1471 at Milan, and this was followed by editions at Venice in 1478 and 1482.

Of far greater importance were the writings of Ptolemy. Near the end of the second century he not only brought together in systematic form the ideas of those who had gone before him, but he elaborated and set forth a system of his own. His work thus became a great source of geographical information throughout the twelve centuries that were to follow. The book, however, scarcely had any popular significance before the fifteenth century; for until that time it was locked up within the mysteries of the Greek language. But in 1409, a version in Latin disseminated his views throughout Europe.

In one respect the theories of Ptolemy were exceptionally important in their bearing upon the western discoveries. It was his belief that the further extension of geographical knowledge was to be obtained by pushing the lines of investigation toward the west rather than toward the north or toward the south. It is of significance in the life of Columbus that the first edition of Ptolemy was printed in 1475, and that several other editions were issued from the press before 1492. It is also of interest to note that the views promulgated by the Alexandrian geographer were essentially the views held and advocated by Columbus.

The theologians generally rejected the idea of sphericity. There were, however, some very notable exceptions. The doctrine was positively taught by Saint Isadore of Seville, and was somewhat elaborately set forth by the Venerable Bede. Of still more importance was the unquestioning acceptance of this doctrine by that great protagonist of the faith, Saint Thomas Aquinas. Albertus Magnus, Roger Bacon, and Dante seem also, in a more or less definite form, to have accepted the same doctrine.

In any account, however brief, of the early years of Columbus, a statement should also be made concerning some of the explorers who had performed an important part in pushing out the boundaries of knowledge.

One of the most remarkable of these was John de Mandeville. It is very properly the fashion to regard this audacious romancer as one of the most unscrupulous of all explorers. It is certain that he did not see a quarter or perhaps even a tenth part of the things which he affects to describe. But in spite of all these characteristics, there is one passage in the book that can hardly fail to have made a deep impression on the mind of Columbus. In this remarkable passage the author relates, in the quaint language of the time, how he himself came to the conclusion that the earth was a sphere. His words are, —

"In the north the south lodestar is not seen; and in the south, the north is not seen.... By which say you certainly that men may environ all the earth, as well under as above, and turn again to his country, and always find men as well as in this country. . . . For ye witten well that they that turn toward the Antarctic, be straight feet against feet of them that dwell under the transmontayne, as well as we and they that dwell under us be feet against feet."

Of still more importance in shaping directly or indirectly the opinions of Columbus was the great work of Marco Polo. This Venetian traveller, after spending many years in China and Japan, and having the best of opportunities for observation, published the great work on which his reputation as a traveller and writer is founded. He not only described with considerable minuteness the countries which he visited, but he pictured, though with gross exaggerations, the great wealth of many of the eastern cities. Columbus supposed that these regions, still in the hands of infidels, could be reached by sailing westward across the Atlantic.

But there was another book that had more influence upon Columbus than all the others; and this was the "Imago Mundi" of Cardinal d'Ailly. It was a kind of encyclopædia of geographical knowledge, in which the author had endeavoured to bring together all the prevailing views in regard to the form of the earth. In the copy of this remarkable book, still preserved in the Columbian Library at Seville, there are still to be seen numerous marginal annotations by Columbus himself. These notes make us absolutely certain that the navigator studied very carefully and early became familiar with the beliefs of all the geographical writers of antiquity and of the Middle Ages.

It is natural to ask the question why, if the earth was known to be spherical, and if the compass was already in existence, voyages of discovery were so long delayed? If one looks at the geographical works of the time, one sees everywhere taught the notion that the unknown regions were peopled with monsters ready to devour any who approached. One of the pictures in the Nuremberg Chronicle, for illustration, represents the Atlantic as filled with monsters so huge as to be able and ready to lift any ship easily upon its back and dash it to destruction. The Arabs believed and taught that in the torrid zone the moisture was so much sucked up by the heat of the sun that the residue was impervious to the passage of ships. Popular credulity everywhere seemed to gain the mastery over science. The early Anglo-Saxon scholars believed that the earth was a globe ; but in spite of all their teaching, we find in an early Anglo-Saxon tract, intended to convey abstruse information in the form of a dialogue, the following question and answer : —

" *Question :* Tell me, my son, why the sun is so red in the evening ?

"*Answer :* Because it looketh down upon hell."

It must be conceded that this doctrine was sufficiently discouraging to western navigation.

It should not, however, be forgotten that while views concerning the sphericity of the earth were gradually making their impression, geographical knowledge was extending itself through the efforts of explorers. The boldest adventurers were gradually pressing their way into the far north. The inhabitants of Iceland — perhaps from their geographical isolation — were especially adventurous. Within the present century the evidence has been made complete that America was visited and explored in the eleventh century, and that accounts of these explorations in detail became a part of the national literature. But Iceland was so isolated from the rest of Europe that these explorations seem to have made no impression, even if they were at all known. The first allusion to the discovery of Amer-

ica by the Scandinavians ever printed was that of
Adam von Bremen, in his work issued from the press
at Copenhagen in 1579.   Although the work had
been in manuscript for centuries, there is no evidence that these explorations made any impression
upon the literature or knowledge of the time.   If
Columbus visited Iceland, it is probable that he became acquainted with the traditions of these western
voyages.   It is of course possible that he obtained
positive information from the stories that may have
been current among the seafaring men of Iceland
in the fifteenth century.   But the matter is left in
doubt by the fact that no such knowledge was ever
revealed by Columbus after his return ; and it hardly
seems probable that he would have kept such an
item of information locked up in his own brain at a
time when he was trying to bring every argument
to bear upon the Portuguese and Spanish courts.

While these numerous intellectual purveyors were
bringing to the mind of Columbus their varied stores
of information, an event occurred which must have
had a powerful influence in shaping and intensifying
his purpose.

In the year 1474 there was living at Florence the
venerable astronomer and geographer Toscanelli.
This eminent savant, now seventy-eight years of age,
after having enjoyed the honours of connection with
nearly all the learned societies of that day, had been
greatly interested in the recently published book of
Marco Polo.   From the account given by this Venetian traveller, Toscanelli had arrived at certain inter-

esting views in regard to the size of the earth. He
had satisfied himself that the open water between
western Europe and eastern Asia could be crossed
in a voyage of not more than three thousand miles.
The letters of Toscanelli have been preserved, and
they form a most interesting part of the history of
this period. We cannot quote from them at any
length, but the importance of the correspondence
is sufficient to justify a concise statement of the particular significance of the letters.

In the first place, in one of the letters, dated in
1474, Toscanelli says that he had already written to
the king of Portugal, urging upon him the practicability of reaching Japan and China by sailing directly
west. He had accompanied this statement, moreover, with a map showing what, in his opinion, would
be found in the course of the proposed voyage.
Unfortunately, the original map of Toscanelli, so far
as we know, has not been preserved. Copies of it,
which we may presume to be substantially accurate,
however, enable us to form a sufficient impression
as to the general nature of his geographical views.
He had no conception of another continent. On
the contrary, he believed that the eastern part of
Asia, excepting as it was fringed with Cipango
(Japan) and other islands, presented its broad and
hospitable front to any navigator bold enough to sail
two or three thousand miles directly west from Portugal or Spain. These beliefs are important, because
they are the identical ones afterward held by Columbus, not only at the time of his first voyage, but
also even until the day of his death.

Another fact indicated in the Toscanelli letters is the desire expressed by Columbus, showing clearly that as early as 1474, three years before the reputed visit to Iceland, he had formed a definite purpose, if possible, to visit and explore the unknown regions of the east by sailing west.

Another peculiarity of Toscanelli's letters relates to the wealth of the countries to be explored. On this point he not only refers to Marco Polo, but also speaks of the descriptions given by an ambassador in the time of Pope Eugenius IV. He says: " I was a great deal in his company, and he gave me descriptions of the munificence of his king, and of the immense rivers in that territory, which contained, as he stated, two hundred cities with marble bridges upon the banks of a single stream." " The city of Quinsay," Toscanelli continues, " is thirty-five leagues in circuit, and it contains ten large marble bridges, built upon immense columns of singular magnificence." Of Cipango, he says: " This island possesses such an abundance of precious stones and metals that the temples and royal palaces are covered with plates of gold."

We have now seen — briefly, it is true, but perhaps with sufficient fulness — how Columbus in various ways had received his education. If called upon to sum up the impressions that he had gained in the course of his experience at Genoa and Lisbon before 1484, the result would be something like the following: First, he acquired a very definite and positive belief in the sphericity of the earth. Secondly, through Toscanelli, Cardinal d'Ailly, and others, he had likewise received an equally definite and positive impression that the size of the earth was much less than it actually is. His belief was that Japan would be reached by sailing west a distance not greater than the distance which actually intervenes between Portugal and the eastern coasts of America. In the third place, these beliefs were confirmed by certain vague reports of sailors that had been driven to the far west, and by such articles as had been thrown by the waters upon the islands lying west of Portugal and northern Africa.

What may be called the approaches to the discovery of America were, in their general characteristics, not unlike those which have generally preceded other great discoveries and inventions. Seldom in the history of the human race has the conception and the consummation of a great discovery been the product of a single brain. The final achievement is ordinarily only the culminating act of the more logical mind and the more dauntless courage. Such was the case with Columbus. The more one becomes familiar with the thought and the enterprise of the fifteenth century, the more clearly one sees how impossible it would have been for America to have long remained undiscovered, even if there had been no Columbus. We shall hereafter see how a Portuguese fleet, in the year 1500, when sailing for Good Hope, and with no thought of a western continent, was driven by storms to the coast of Brazil. But none of these facts should detract from the credit of Columbus. The great man of such a time is the one who shows that he knows the law of development, and, bringing all possible knowledge to his service, works, with a lofty courage and an unflagging persistency and enthusiasm, for the object of his devotion in accordance with the strict laws of historical sequence. Such was the method of Columbus. Others, perhaps, were as familiar with all the geographical facts and theories with which he had so long been storing his mind; others even saw as clearly the conclusions to which these facts and theories so distinctly pointed: but he alone, of all the men of his generation, was possessed with the lofty enthusiasm, the ardent prescience, the unhasting and unresting courage, that were the harbingers of glorious success.

CHAPTER II.

ATTEMPTS TO SECURE ASSISTANCE.

An enterprise so vast and hazardous as that proposed by Columbus was not likely to receive adequate assistance from any private benefactor. Though the Portuguese had long been considered daring navigators, no one of them had yet undertaken an expedition in any way comparable in point of novelty and boldness with that now proposed. The explorers of Prince Henry had skirted along the coasts of Africa, following out lines of discovery that had already been somewhat plainly marked out. But what Columbus now proposed was the bolder course of cutting loose from old traditions and methods, and sailing directly west into an unknown space. Capital was even more conservative and timid in the fifteenth century than it is at the present time ; and therefore great expeditions were much more dependent upon governmental assistance. It was not singular, therefore, that Columbus found himself obliged to seek for governmental support and protection.

But in this, as in so many other details in the life of Columbus, it is impossible at the present time to be confident that we have ascertained the exact truth. Many of the early accounts are conflicting; and not a few of the prevailing impressions are founded on evidence that will not bear the test of critical examination. For example, nearly all of the historians assert that Columbus made application for assistance to the governments of Genoa and Venice.

The only authority for belief that the Admiral applied to Genoa is a statement of Ramusio, who affirms that he received his information from Peter Martyr. In the course of the narrative he says that when the application was rejected, Columbus, at the age of forty, determined to go to Portugal. Unfortunately, to our acceptance of this circumstantial statement there are several very serious obstacles. In the first place, no authority for such an assertion can be found in all the writings of Peter Martyr. Again, the archives of Genoa have been thoroughly explored in vain for any evidence of such an application. But most important of all, the assertion, if true, would prove that Columbus was born as early as 1430. We should also be obliged to infer that two of his children by the same mother differed in age by at least thirty-six years. The impression that Columbus made application for assistance to Genoa may therefore safely be dismissed as apocryphal.

The evidence in regard to an application to Venice, though less positive in its nature, is also inconclusive. The Venetian historian Carlo Antonio Marin, whose history of Venetian commerce was not published till the year 1800, was the first to give currency to the story. His authority is this. He says that Francesco

Pesaro said to him some ten or twelve years before, —
that is, about 1780, — that in making some researches
in the archives of the Council of Ten, he had seen
and read a letter of Columbus making application to
the Venetian Government for assistance. But although diligent search has since been made at two
different times throughout the archives for the years
between 1470 and 1492, no trace of such a letter has
ever been found. It is possible that this important
document may have been destroyed when, just before
the preliminaries of Leoben, in May, 1797, a mob
invaded the hall of the Council of Ten and dispersed
such of the papers as could be found. But until some
further evidence comes to light, it must be considered doubtful whether application to Venice was ever
made.

In regard to applications to Portugal, England, and
France, the evidence is less incomplete, though here,
too, we meet with not a few conflicting statements.

In one of his letters to the Spanish sovereigns
Columbus says : "For twenty-seven years I had been
trying to get recognition, but at the end of that period all my projects were turned to ridicule. . . . But
notwithstanding this fact," he continues, "I pressed
on with zeal, and responded to France, Portugal, and
England that I reserved for the king and queen those
countries and those domains." Elsewhere he says :
"In order to serve your Highnesses, I listened to
neither England nor Portugal nor France, whose
princes wrote me letters which your Highnesses can
see in the hands of Dr. Villalono."

There is another bit of evidence on this subject that is not less interesting. On the 19th of March, 1493, the Duke of Medina Celi wrote to Cardinal de Mendoza asking that he might be permitted to send vessels every year to trade in America, and urging as a reason for this special favor the fact that he had prevented Columbus from going to the service of France and had held him to the service of Spain, at a time when he had opportunities for going elsewhere.

But as if to prevent us from being too confident that we have arrived at the exact truth, Columbus in another of his letters gives us a statement which, if it stood alone, would seem to prove that John II. not only made no offer, but stubbornly refused all assistance. He says: " The king of Portugal refused with blindness to second me in my projects of maritime discovery, for God closed his eyes, ears, and all his senses, so that in fourteen years I was not able to make him listen to what I advanced."

From this it would seem to be certain that the offer of Portugal alluded to in the letter above quoted was not made earlier than 1487, fully two years after Columbus had arrived in Spain.

That Columbus's application was made as early as 1474, the Toscanelli correspondence is sufficient proof. But the moment was not auspicious. John II., who was then reigning, appears to have had no aversion to giving aid to such an enterprise ; but he was involved in expensive wars, and any additional drafts upon the treasury would have met with exceptional difficulty.

But there was another reason that ought not to be overlooked. The recent maritime history of Portugal had given the Government a very natural feeling of self-reliance. The extraordinary efforts and successes of Prince Henry had borne fruit. Portugal had not only raised up a large number of skilful explorers, but had attracted to Lisbon all the great navigators of the time. Diego Cam and Behaim had gone beyond the Congo. Affonso de Aviero had visited the kingdom of Benin, and Pedro de Covilham had advanced to Calicut by way of the Red Sea. Affonso de Pavia had reached Abyssinia, and Bartholomew Diaz was at the point of doubling the Cape of Good Hope. Thus a vast number of expeditions had been sent out, not only to the coasts of Africa, but also to the open sea. In 1513 De Mafra testified that the king of Portugal had sent out two exploring expeditions that had returned without results. In view of all these facts the refusal of the Portuguese monarch might easily be explained on the ground of anterior engagements to his own subjects.

But notwithstanding the assurances of Columbus himself, it is certain that there was no absolute refusal. On the contrary, there is positive proof that the king took the matter into most careful consideration. He not only listened with attention to the scheme, but, if we may believe the testimony of Fernando, gave a qualified promise of support. Columbus accepted an invitation of the monarch to unfold his hypothesis in reference to the extent of Asia, the splendors of the region described by Marco Polo, the shortness of the distance across the Atlantic, and the entire practicability of reaching the East Indies by a directly westward course.

Of this interview we have two accounts, one written by the Admiral's son Fernando, and the other by De Barros, the Portuguese historiographer. According to Fernando, his father supported the prosecution of the plan by such excellent reasons that the king did not hesitate to give his consent. But when Columbus, being a man of lofty and noble ideals, demanded honorable titles and rewards, the king found the matter quite beyond the means then at his disposal. De Barros, on the other hand, assures us that the seeming acquiescence of the king was simply his manner of answerihg what he regarded as the unreasonable importunities of Columbus. He considered the navigator as a vainglorious man, fond of displaying his abilities and given to fantastic notions, such as those respecting the island of Cipango. According to this same authority, it was but another way of getting rid of Columbus that the king referred the whole subject to a committee of the Council for Geographical Affairs.

It is said that councils of war never fight, and that advisory boards regard the promoters of new schemes as their natural enemies. The committee to whom the king referred the proposal of Columbus was made up of two Jewish physicians and a bishop. Although the physicians, Roderigo and Joseph, were reputed as the most able cosmographers of the realm, they had not much hesitation in deciding that the project was extravagant and visionary. With this judgment the

ecclesiastical member of the council seems to have
agreed.

The king, however, as if unwilling to lose any valuable opportunity, does not appear to have been satisfied with this answer. As the story goes, he convoked
his royal council, and asked their advice whether to
adopt this new route, or to pursue that which had
already been opened.

Von Concelos, the historian of King John II., has
given a graphic account of the discussion held before this council. The Bishop of Ceuta, the same
important dignitary that had been a member of the
committee of three, opposed this scheme in a cool
and deliberate speech. The opposite side was presented by Dom Pedro de Meneses with so much
eloquence and power that the impression he made
quite surpassed that of the colder reasonings of the
bishop. What followed was apparently prompted by
a consciousness that the advocates of the scheme were
likely to be successful. The bishop now proposed a
very unworthy scheme. He asked that Columbus
might be kept in suspense while a vessel should be
secretly despatched by the king to discover whether
there was any foundation for his theory. The king
appears not to have been above the adoption of so
base a proposition. Columbus was required to furnish for the consideration of the council a plan of
his proposed voyage, together with the charts and
maps with which he intended to guide his course. A
small vessel was despatched, ostensibly to the Cape
de Verde islands, but with private instructions to pro-

ceed on the route pointed out by Columbus. The officer had no heart in the enterprise, and it was a complete failure. Sailing westward for several days, they encountered storms, and the sailors, losing their courage, returned to ridicule the project as impossible.

When these facts came to be known, they produced a very natural impression on the mind of Columbus. Disgusted with the treatment he had received from the Portuguese, he quitted Lisbon for Spain at a date which cannot be determined with precision, but probably in the latter part of the year 1484 or in the early part of 1485. His departure had to be secret, lest he should be detained either by the king or his creditors. Color is given to the supposition that he was under grave charges of some kind by the fact that King John, when, some years later, inviting him to return to Portugal, deemed it necessary to insure him "against arrest on account of any process, civil or criminal, that might be pending against him."

Now, in considering all these accounts, it is not difficult to imagine that in his efforts to promote his great schemes, Columbus had been kept in poverty. But the reasons for his leaving in secret, and even his movements on leaving Portugal, are involved in uncertainty.

It has also very often been held by modern historians that Columbus, immediately after entering Spain, found his way to the monastery of La Rabida, near Palos. The authority for this belief, moreover, is nothing less than a circumstantial account given by

Fernando. But the assertion has been proved to be incorrect. In the trial of 1513, in which Diego Columbus attempted to establish certain claims against the Government, two witnesses gave sworn testimony in regard to the meeting at La Rabida. This testimony is still to be seen in the records of the trial; and the details of the evidence make it almost absolutely certain that the visit of Columbus to that famous monastery was not when he first entered Spain in 1484 or 1485, but as late as September or October of 1491.

Of another interesting effort, however, we have more positive information. It was probably before leaving Portugal that he despatched his brother Bartholomew to make application to the king of England. But whatever the date of the application, it was not successful. Whether the presentation of the case was made orally or in writing can perhaps never be determined. It is known that he was in England for a considerable period; but no trace of the application itself has ever been found in the English authorities of the time. After remaining in England probably until 1488, Bartholomew went to France, where he remained until 1494. Though it seems probable that he received some encouragement at the French court, even the probability rests upon no documentary evidence except the assertion of Columbus, already quoted. That hopes were held out, may perhaps be inferred from the fact that when, almost at the last moment, Columbus turned his back upon the Spanish court, he decided to go to France.

As to the course pursued by Columbus after he reached Spain, there is also some uncertainty. This is owing to the impossibility of reconciling some of the statements of Fernando with many of the other statements found in the contemporaneous records. If the narrative of the son in regard to the course of the father is followed, the student will find himself in a labyrinth of difficulties. Fernando would have us believe that immediately after entering Spain his father went to the court of Medina Celi, and a little later had his famous experience at the monastery of La Rabida. But it is impossible to reconcile such a statement with the subsequent current of events. We know, as we shall presently see, that Columbus was two years in the house of the Duke of Medina Celi, and that at the end of that period he took a letter of introduction and commendation to Cardinal Mendoza at the court of Ferdinand and Isabella. We know also that the visit to La Rabida was the cause of a letter being written which induced Columbus to take that journey to the court, which resulted in the ultimate adoption of his cause. The letter of Medina, moreover, assured the monarch that Columbus was on the point of taking his enterprise to the court of France. This assertion appears to be altogether incompatible with the supposition that the abode of Columbus with Medina Celi was in the early part of his residence in Spain. Not to present a tedious array of irreconcilable details, it is perhaps enough to say that if the statement of Fernando is once rejected, the way is, for the most part, easy and clear. If we once adopt the supposition that the abode with Medina Celi began in 1489, and that the visit to La Rabida was in September or October of 1491, we shall rest on the authority of Las Casas, and shall find that the difficulties in the way of accounting for the movements of Columbus are chiefly removed. Against this supposition, moreover, there is no evidence except the statement of Fernando, published not less than eighty years after the events it purports to describe.

With this explanation let us endeavour to point out the course of Columbus in the light of the original evidence.

Before we can understand the course that was taken, we must glance at the general condition of Spain.

The modern Inquisition was established in Castile by royal decree in September of 1480. It proceeded with so much energy that in the course of the following year, it is estimated that no less than two thousand persons were burned at the stake. The queen appears to have had some scruples in regard to this wholesale slaughter; but these were allayed by Pope Sixtus the Fourth, who encouraged her by an audacious reference to the example of Christ, who, he said, established his kingdom by the destruction of idolatry. This teaching was effective. In the autumn of 1483 the terrible Torquemada was appointed Inquisitor-General, and clothed with full powers to reorganize the Holy Office and exterminate heresy. From that time until the end of this inquisitor's term of office, according to the estimation of Llorente, the annual number of persons condemned to torture was more than six thousand, and in the course of the whole period more than ten thousand were burned alive. The success of the Inquisition in Castile was so satisfactory that Ferdinand resolved to introduce it into Aragon. Notwithstanding a remonstrance of the Cortes, the *auto-da-fé*, with all its horrors, was set up at Saragossa in the month of May, 1485. The Aragonese, despairing of any other way of protecting themselves, resolved upon an appalling act of violence. Arbues, the most odious of the inquisitors, was attacked by a band of conspirators and assassinated on his knees before the great altar of the cathedral, in a manner that reminds us of the death of Thomas à Becket at Canterbury. The whole kingdom was consequently thrown into turmoil.

But there were other causes of anxiety. This very year the prevalence of the plague added to the general solicitude. In some of the southern districts of the kingdom the ravages of the pestilence showed not only the appalling condition of the people, but also the necessity of governmental assistance. In several of the cities as many as eight or ten thousand of the inhabitants were swept away. In Seville alone the number that perished this very year was no less than fifteen thousand.

Just at this juncture, moreover, the coin of the realm was adulterated, and a fatal shock was given to commercial credit. The people very generally refused to receive the debased money in payment of debts. Prices of ordinary articles rose to such a height as to be above the reach of the poorer classes of the community. Great destitution prevailed, and the resources of the Government were put to the severest strain. Even if there had been no other tax upon the treasures of the king and queen, the time would not have been propitious for an application like that of Columbus.

But there was another and a still more important reason. For more than three years the terrible war against the Moors had been taxing the resources of the united armies of Ferdinand and Isabella. When the Genoese navigator entered Spain, the court was making active preparations for a vigorous continuation of that titanic struggle. The rival kings of Granada had formed a coalition that now called for the most prompt and vigorous action. The headquarters of the king and queen were established at Cordova, where the active operations in the field could be most easily and successfully directed; and all the resources of Castile and Aragon were called into requisition to meet these emergencies in the famous contest of the Cross against the Crescent.

No one can fairly judge either of the generosity or of the justice of the monarchs in dealing with Columbus, without taking into consideration all these prior obligations. At the very moment when this enterprising navigator applied for assistance, there must have arisen to the minds of Ferdinand and Isabella a vivid consciousness of the ominous ferment caused by the work of the Inquisition; of the suffering occasioned by the plague; of the starvation that everywhere appealed for help in consequence of the

debasement of the currency and the rise in prices ;
and, finally, of the all-absorbing necessity of bringing
every resource of the country to bear upon the ending of this terrible war against Granada. Nor can it
be forgotten that the war was still to make its demands upon the country for six years. In view of all
the facts, it is difficult to imagine a concurrence of
circumstances more unfavorable to the application.
The monarchs could not have been justly blamed if
they had summarily declared that a granting of the
application was impossible. And yet, that they were
unwilling to reject the application outright, the course
of events abundantly shows.

Columbus, in a letter dated the 14th of January,
1493, says that seven years the twentieth of that
month had rolled away since he entered the service
of the Spanish monarchs. This exact statement, corroborated in substance as it is by others, would seem
to fix the date of his entering the Spanish service as
the 20th of January, 1486. What the nature of this
service was, cannot now be determined. Nor do we
know whether from this time he received pecuniary
support. The first record of such assistance, indeed
the first authentic documentary evidence of his being
in Spain, occurs in an entry in the books of the royal
treasurer for the 5th of May, 1487. Under this date
is found the following entry : " To-day paid three
thousand maravedis [about twenty dollars] to Christopher Columbus, stranger, who is here employed in
certain things for their Highnesses, under the direction of Alphonso de Quintanilla, by order of the

bishop." In one of his letters to Ferdinand, Columbus says : "As soon as your Highness had knowledge of my desire [to visit the Indies], you protected me and honored me with favors."

While there is nothing in these assertions to indicate the exact date when Columbus began to receive pecuniary assistance, we are justified in the inference that it was in January of 1486.

There is no evidence, however, that Columbus presented himself at the Spanish capital before the following spring. Surely the times must have seemed to him inauspicious. The monarchs had established themselves at Cordova as the most convenient place for the headquarters of the army. Early in the year, the king marched off to lay siege to the Moorish city of Illora, while Isabella remained at Cordova to forward the necessary troops and supplies. A little later we find both monarchs, in person, carrying on the siege of Moclin. Scarcely had they returned to Cordova, however, when they were obliged to set out for Galicia to suppress the rebellion of the Count of Lemos.

During this summer of military turmoil, Columbus remained at Cordova vainly waiting for an opportunity to present his cause. Fortunately he was not without some encouragement; for he had gained the favor of Alonzo de Quintanilla, whose guest he became, and through whom he made the acquaintance of Geraldini, the preceptor of the younger children of Ferdinand and Isabella.

When the monarchs repaired to the northern town

of Salamanca for the winter, Columbus also went
thither with his friends Quintanilla and Geraldini.
Here it was that the cause of the explorer first had a
formal hearing.

At this audience it is not probable that Queen Isabella was present; at least, the only part of the discussion taken by the monarchs seems to have been
that of the king. It is said that Columbus unfolded
his scheme with entire self-possession. He appears to
have been neither dazzled nor daunted; for in a letter
to the sovereign, in 1501, he declares that on this occasion " he felt himself kindled as with a fire from on
high, and considered himself as an agent chosen by
Heaven to accomplish a grand design."

But so important a matter as that now urged upon
the sovereigns was not to be entered upon lightly or
in haste. However willing the king may have been
to be the promoter of discoveries far more important
than those which had shed glory upon Portugal, he
was too cool and shrewd a man to decide a matter
hastily which involved so many scientific principles.
Of the details of what followed we have no authentic
account. After more than a hundred years had
passed away, and the glory of the discovery had come
in some measure to be appreciated, the claim was
set up that a congress or junta of learned men was
called together, and that the whole subject was submitted to their consideration. The account, however,
is accompanied with many suspicious circumstances.
The historian Remesal was a Dominican monk and
a member of the monastery of St. Stephen at Sala-

manca, where, it is said, the junta was held. In his narrative he claims that the ecclesiastical members, for the most part monks of St. Stephen, listened with approval to the presentation of the case, while those who might be called the scientific members strenuously opposed it. This statement, which is the basis of Irving's account, is not only inherently improbable, but is supported by no contemporaneous evidence whatever. The absence of such evidence, moreover, is enough to condemn the whole story. The records of the monastery, which are supposed to be complete, contain no reference to any such meeting. Las Casas, himself a Dominican, would have been sure to introduce the account into his narrative if it had rested upon any basis of fact. He makes no allusion to any such meeting, and we are forced to conclude that the story was fabricated for ecclesiastical purposes. But although no such formal meeting was ever held, there is evidence that Ferdinand obtained, in an informal way, the opinions of some of the most learned men of the time.

The city of Salamanca, where this order was issued, seemed in every way favourable for such a hearing; for at this ancient capital was situated one of the most renowned universities of Spain. It is difficult to suppose that the professors of that venerable institution were not familiar with the latest theories in regard to the sphericity of the earth; but notwithstanding this fact, Columbus had to confront, not only the prudent conservatism of learning, but also the obstinate conservatism of the Church. The faculties were made up partly of ecclesiastics, and partly of others who soon became fully imbued with the ecclesiastical spirit. It was at a time when there was no more thought of tolerating heresy than there was of tolerating arson. The Inquisition, as we have just seen, had recently been established. In both the king and the queen an ardent religious zeal was united with great political and military skill, as well as great personal popularity. Heresy was the most dangerous of crimes, and the strictest adherence to traditional doctrines was encouraged by all the considerations of loyalty, of interest, and of prudence. To the dark colours in which heresy was painted by the Church in the fifteenth century, a still deeper hue was now added by the horrors of the Moorish wars. It is therefore easy to explain why the people of Spain surpassed the people of other countries in the fervour of religious intolerance. Columbus was obliged to plead the cause of his departure from traditional methods in an atmosphere charged with all these predispositions, prejudices, and motives. By the vulgar crowd the navigator had persistently been scoffed at as a visionary; but with something of the hopeful enthusiasm of an adventurer, he had steadily maintained the belief that it was only necessary to meet a body of enlightened men to insure their conversion to his cause.

But his hopefulness was destined to be disabused. We can well believe that his project appeared in a somewhat unfavourable light before the learned men of the day. To them he was simply an obscure navigator, and a foreigner at that, depending upon nothing more than the force of the reasons he might be able to present. Some of them, no doubt, looked upon him simply as an adventurer, while others were disposed to manifest their impatience at any doctrinal innovation. The predominance of opinion seemed to intrench itself in the belief that after so many cosmographers and navigators had been studying and exploring the globe for centuries, it was simply an absurd presumption to suppose that any new discoveries of importance were now to be made.

The discussion, almost at the very first, was taken out of the domain of science. Instead of attempting to present astronomical and geographical objections to the proposed voyage, the objectors assailed the scheme with citations from the Bible and from the Fathers of the Church. The book of Genesis, the Psalms of David, the Prophets, and the Gospels were all put upon the witness-stand and made to testify to the impossibility of success. Saint Chrysostom, Saint Augustine, Lactantius, Saint Jerome, Saint Gregory, and a host of others, were cited as confirmatory witnesses. Philosophical and mathematical demonstrations received no consideration. The simple proposition of Columbus that the earth was spherical was met with texts of Scripture in a manner that was worthy of Father Jasper.

These various presentations, however, were by no means in vain; for there was far from unanimity of opinion. There were a few who admitted that

Saint Thomas Aquinas and Saint Isadore might be right in believing the earth to be globular in form; though even these were inclined to deny that circumnavigation was possible. It is a pleasure to note, however, that there was one conspicuous exception to the general current of opposition and resistance. Whether dating from this period we do not know, but it is certain that an early interest was taken in the cause by Diego de Deza, a learned friar of the order of St. Dominic, who afterward became archbishop of Seville, one of the highest ecclesiastical dignitaries of the realm. Deza appears to have risen quite above the limitations of mere ecclesiastical lore; for he not only took a generous interest in the cause of the explorer, but he seconded and encouraged his efforts with all the means at his command. Perhaps it was by his efforts that so deep an impression was made on the most learned men of the conference. However this may have been, the ignorant and the prejudiced remained obstinate in their opposition, and so the season at Salamanca passed away without bringing the monarchs to any decision.

After the winter of 1486–87, there occurred a long and painful period of delays. In the following spring the court departed from Salamanca and went to Cordova to prepare for the memorable campaign against Malaga. Columbus accompanied the expedition in the vain hope that there would be an opportunity for a further hearing. At one time when the Spanish armies were encamped on the hills and plains surrounding the beleaguered city, Columbus

was summoned to court.; but amid the din of a
terrible contest there was no place for a calm consideration of the great maritime project. The summer was full of incident and peril. At one time the
king was surprised and nearly cut off by the craft
of the old Moorish monarch;. at another a Moorish
fanatic attempted to assassinate both king and queen,
only to be cut to pieces after he had wounded the
prince of Portugal and the Marchioness de Moya,
supposing them to be Ferdinand and Isabella.

But it is easy to imagine that this seemingly untoward event contributed to help on the cause of
Columbus. The Marchioness de Moya had warmly
espoused his cause, and the attempt upon her life
can hardly have failed to appeal to the interest of
Queen Isabella.

Malaga surrendered in August, and the king and
queen almost immediately returned to Cordova. The
pestilence, however, very soon made that old city an
unsafe abode. For a while the court was in what
might be called the turmoil of migration. At one
time it was in Valladolid, at another in Saragossa, at
another in Medina de Campo. But during all this
period its ardent business was the pressing forward
of the Spanish armies into the Moorish territories.
As every reader of Irving knows, the ground was
stubbornly contested, inch by inch. Columbus remained for the most part with the army; but he
sought in vain for the quiet necessary for a dis-
passionate hearing.

It could hardly have been otherwise. Ferdinand

and Isabella have often been reproached with needless delays in the matter of rendering the required
assistance ; but such a reproach cannot be justified.
The custom of the time sanctioned, even if it did
not require, that the court should accompany the
military camp. The Government was not only at the
head of the army, but it was actually and continu-
ously in the field. All other questions were absorbed
by the military interests of the moment; and it
would have been singular indeed, if, in such a situation, the resources of the treasury had been called
upon to subsidize an expedition that as yet had been
unable to secure the approval of the learned men
who had been asked to consider its merits. It would
be difficult to show that the course taken by the
monarchs was not both wise and natural. The
period of the war was a fit time in which to ascertain
the merits of the proposal ; and if after the contest
should be brought to an end, the reports should be
found favorable, the expedition could be fitted out
with such assistance as might comport with the condition of the treasury and the necessities of the case.

But, on the other hand, it was not singular that
Columbus was at this time wearied and discouraged
by the delays. The end of the war was still involved
in great uncertainty, and there was no assurance that
even at the return of peace his proposals would receive the royal approval and support. It was not
unnatural, then, that he began to think of applying
elsewhere for assistance. In the spring of 1488 he
wrote to the king of Portugal, asking permission to

return to that country. The reply, received on the 20th of March, not only extended the desired invitation, but also gave him the significant assurance of protection against any suits of a criminal or civil nature that might be pending against him. About the same time he seems also to have received a letter from Henry VII. of England, inviting him to that country, and holding out certain vague promises of encouragement. Though this letter was doubtless the fruit of the efforts made by his brother Bartholomew, there is no evidence that Columbus ever thought favourably of accepting the invitation. Why it was that he delayed going to Portugal until late in the autumn cannot be determined with certainty. It is, however, not difficult to conjecture. Harrisse has found in the treasury-books memoranda of small amounts of money paid to Columbus from time to time during his stay in the vicinity of the Spanish court. Ferdinand and Isabella were sufficiently interested in the project to be unwilling that he should carry his proposition to another monarch. At least, they were anxious that he should not commit himself elsewhere until they should have had opportunity to examine into the project with care; and then, at the close of the war, if it seemed best, they would give him the needed support. Accordingly, elaborate preparations for a new hearing were at once made. No less than three royal orders were issued, — one summoning Columbus to a council of learned men at Seville; one directing the city authorities to provide lodgings for the navigator, as for an officer of the government; another commanding the magistrates of the cities along the way to furnish accommodations for him and for his attendants.

These orders were all carried out; but the conference was postponed, and finally interrupted by the opening of the campaign for the summer. The annals of Seville contain a statement that in this campaign Columbus was found fighting and " giving proofs of the distinguishing valor which accompanied his wisdom and his lofty desires." What we positively know of the course of events may be summed up as follows. On the 3d of July, 1487, he received the second stipend in money. At the end of the following August we find him at the siege of Malaga. In the winter of 1487–88 he was at Cordova, when his relations with Beatriz Enriquez resulted in the birth of his son Fernando on the 15th of August, 1488. On the 16th of June of this year Columbus received the third allowance of money. Early in the spring he had asked for permission to return to Portugal, and the letter granting his request bears date of the 20th of March. The journey was not undertaken, however, until after the birth of his son. When he went, and how long he remained in Portugal, are uncertain; for the only positive proof that he took the journey at all is a memorandum in his own handwriting, dated at Lisbon in December of 1488. It is, however, interesting to note that this memorandum, made in his copy of Cardinal d'Ailly's " Imago Mundi," calls attention to the return of Diaz from his voyage to the Cape of Good Hope. It is, however, definitely ascertained that he returned in the spring of 1489; for on the 12th of May of that year an order was issued to all the authorities of the cities through which he passed, to furnish him all needed support and assistance at the royal expense.

The fact that this is the last time that Columbus figures in the order-books of the treasury has led Harrisse to infer that the navigator saw no immediate chance of success, and so for a time abstained from the further pressing of his suit.

We are thus brought to the autumn of 1489, when Columbus, seeing little reason for hope, but still not so discouraged as to abandon his cause, formed an acquaintance which proved to be of incalculable value. How the acquaintance came about, we have no means of knowing. The authorities are so at variance with one another on the subject that there has been much difference of opinion as to the time when the acquaintance was formed. Irving and the larger number of modern writers have supposed that the events which resulted from this connection occurred soon after Columbus entered Spain. Harrisse, however, has pointed out with great acumen the difficulties in the way of accepting this supposition, and has established at least an overwhelming probability that the residence of the navigator with the Duke of Medina Celi extended from the early months of 1490 to the end of 1491.

At the beginning of the fifteenth century Spain was still very largely made up of principalities that were practically independent. Two of these were possessed and governed by the Dukes of Medina Sidonia and Medina Celi. In the wars against Naples, as well as in the long struggle against the Moors, these noblemen fitted out expeditions and conducted campaigns with something like regal independence and magnitude. They lived in royal splendour, and dispensed a royal hospitality. As their vast states lay along the sea-coast at the southwest of Spain, where they had ships and ports, as well as hosts of retainers, it is not singular that this enterprising refugee from the Spanish camp found his way into their domains.

With Medina Sidonia, Columbus seems to have had no special success, though the nobleman is reported to have given him many interviews. The very splendour of the project may have thrown over it such a colouring of improbability as to raise a feeling of distrust. To the hard-headed old hero of so many campaigns, the proposal was simply the undertaking of an Italian visionary.

But upon Medina Celi the navigator made a more favourable impression. Unfortunately, we are dependent for information almost solely upon the statements of the duke. But the narrative has the air of probability. He says that he entertained Columbus for two years at his house. At one time he had gone so far as to set apart and fit out several of his own ships for the purposes of an expedition; but it suddenly occurred to him that an enterprise of such magnitude and importance should go forth under no less sanction than that of the sovereign power. Finding that

Columbus in his disappointment had decided to turn
next to the king of France, the duke determined to
write to Queen Isabella and recommend him strongly
to her favourable consideration. Among other things,
he wrote that the glory of such an enterprise, if successful, should be kept by the monarchs of Spain.
Of the kind favour of the duke there can be no
question; for the letter of introduction carried by
Columbus is still preserved. This important document not only commends the bearer to favourable
consideration, but it also asks that in case the favour
should be granted, the duke himself might have the
privilege of a share in the enterprise, and that the
expedition might be fitted out at his own port of
St. Marie, as a recompense for having waived his
privilege in favour of the grant.

During the next year and a half the prospect
seemed in no way more propitious. Columbus, even
though he now had the support of Medina Celi, must
have been reduced to something like desperation.
The court was making preparations for a final campaign against Granada, with a full determination never
to raise the siege until the Spanish flag should float
above the last Moorish citadel. Columbus knew that
when once the campaign should be entered upon, it
would be vain to expect any attention to his cause.
Accordingly, he pressed for an immediate answer.
The sovereigns called upon the queen's confessor,
Talavera, to obtain the opinions of the scientific men
and to report their decision. This order was com-
plied with; but after due consideration, a majority

decided that the proposed scheme was vain and impossible.

This answer would seem to have been, for the time at least, conclusive; but the men consulted were by no means unanimous. On the contrary, several of the learned members strenuously exerted themselves in favour of the enterprise. Of these the most earnest and influential was the friar Diego de Deza, who, owing to his influential position as tutor of Prince John, had ready access to the royal ear. The matter, therefore, was not peremptorily dismissed. The monarchs, instead of rejecting the application outright, ordered Talavera to inform Columbus that the expense of the war and the cares attending it made it impossible to undertake any new enterprise; but that when peace should be assured, the sovereigns would have leisure and inclination to reconsider the whole question.

Disheartened and indignant at what he considered nothing more than a courtly method of evading and dismissing his suit, Columbus resolved immediately to turn his back upon the Spanish court. For six years he had now pleaded his cause, apparently in vain. Hoping for nothing further, he determined to seek the patronage of the king of France.

It is interesting to note that, taking his boy Diego with him, he made his way to that very seaport town upon which a little later he was to bestow an undying fame by embarking from it on his memorable expedition. Notwithstanding the fact that Medina Celi had given him a home, he must have been reduced to extreme poverty. He seems not only to have travelled on foot, but also to have been under the necessity of begging even for a crust of bread.

Just before he was to reach the port at Palos, Columbus stopped at the gate of the convent of Santa Maria de la Rabida to ask for food and water for himself and his little boy. It happened that the prior of the convent was Juan Parez de Marchena, a friar who had once been the confessor of Queen Isabella. He appears to have had some geographical knowledge; for he at once interested himself in the conversation of Columbus, and was greatly impressed with the grandeur of his views. On hearing that the navigator was to abandon Spain and turn to the court of France, his patriotism was aroused. He not only urged the hospitality of the convent upon the traveller until further advice could be taken, but within a few days he enlisted two or three persons of influence for his cause. One of these was Garcia Fernandez, a physician; another was Martin Alonzo Pinzon, an experienced navigator of Palos. Pinzon, on hearing what was proposed, was so fully convinced of the feasibility of the plan that he offered to bear the expense of the new application, and, if successful, to assist the expedition with his purse and his person.

But it was to the prior of the convent that Columbus was to be most indebted. The result of their several interviews was the determination that the queen's old confessor should make one further appeal. With this end in view, a courier was despatched with a letter. It was successful. After a wearisome journey of fourteen days, the messenger returned with a note summoning Perez to the royal court, then encamped about Granada. At midnight of the same day the prior mounted his mule and set out on his mission of persuasion.

On arriving at the camp, Perez was received with a welcome that gave him great freedom. As the queen's old confessor, he had immediate access to the royal presence, and he pleaded the project of the navigator with fervid enthusiasm. He defended the scientific principles on which it was founded; he urged the unquestionable capacity of Columbus to carry out the undertaking; he pictured not only the advantages that must come from success, but also the glory that would accrue to the Government under whose patronage success should be achieved.

The queen listened with attention. It is interesting to note that the cause was warmly seconded by the queen's favourite, the same Marchioness de Moya whose life had been imperilled by the dagger of the Moorish fanatic. A decision was reached without much delay. The queen not only requested that Columbus might be sent to her, but she gave the messengers a purse to bear the necessary expenses, and to enable the maritime suitor to travel and present himself with decency and comfort.

The successful friar at once returned to the convent, and reported the result of his mission to his waiting friends. Without delay, Columbus exchanged his garb for one suited to the atmosphere of the court, and set out for the royal presence.

In his journal, as quoted by Las Casas, Columbus

tells us that he arrived at Granada in time to see the end of that memorable war. After a struggle of nearly eight hundred years, the Crescent had at length succumbed to the Cross, and the banners of Spain were planted on the highest tower of the Alhambra. The jubilee that followed had all the characteristics of Spanish magnificence. But in these festivities Columbus probably took only the part of an observer. By one of the Spanish historians he is represented as "melancholy and dejected in the midst of general rejoicings."

As soon as the festivities were over, his cause had a hearing. Fernando de Talavera, now elevated to the archbishopric of Granada, was appointed to carry on the negotiations. At the very outset, however, difficulties arose that seemed to be insuperable. Columbus would listen to none but princely conditions. He made the stupendous mistake of demanding that he should be admiral and viceroy over all the countries he might discover. As pecuniary compensation, he also asked for a tenth of all gains either by trade or conquest.

It can hardly be considered singular that the courtiers were indignant at what they regarded as his extravagant requirements. Though Columbus had seen much and hard service at sea, his experience hitherto had not been of a nature to reveal any extraordinary ability. For six years he had been simply a wandering suppliant for royal favour. What he now demanded was to be put into the very highest rank in the realm. As admiral and viceroy he would stand

next to the sovereigns on land, as well as on sea.
What he asked as compensation, though it would
stimulate every temptation to abuse, was not of so
unreasonable a nature. But to promote this obscure
navigator, and a foreigner at that, over all the veterans
who had for perhaps half a century been faithfully
earning recognition, seemed very naturally to the
archbishop preposterous indeed. One of the courtiers observed with a sneer that it was a shrewd arrangement that he proposed, whereby in any event
he would have the honor of the command and the
rank, while he had nothing whatever to lose in case
of failure. Though Columbus, doubtless remember-
ing the offer of Pinzon, offered to furnish one eighth
of the cost, on condition of having one eighth of the
profits, his terms were pronounced inadmissible. The
commission represented to the queen that, even in
case of success, the demands would be exorbitant,
while in case of failure, as evidence of extraordinary
credulity, they would subject the Crown to ridicule.

More than all this, the terms demanded were of
such a nature as to stir the jealousy and hostility of
all the less fortunate naval commanders. Columbus
has been represented by Irving and many of the
other biographers as having shown in these demands
a loftiness of spirit and a firmness of purpose that
are worthy of the highest commendation. But when
one looks at the far-reaching consequences of the
terms insisted upon, one can hardly fail to see in them
the source of very much of the unhappiness and
opposition that followed him throughout his career.

The strenuousness of his terms, by throwing wide open the door to every form of abuse, detracted from his happiness and diminished his claim to greatness.

But Columbus would listen to nothing less than all these conditions. More moderate terms were offered, and such as now seem in every way to have been honourable and advantageous. But all was in vain. ·He would not cede a single point in his demands. The negotiations accordingly had to be broken off. He determined to abandon the court of Spain forever rather than detract one iota from the dignity of the great enterprise he had in view. We are told that, taking leave of his friends, he mounted his mule and sallied forth from Santa Fé, intending immediately to present his cause at the court of France.

But no sooner had he gone than the friends who had ardently supported him were filled with something like consternation. They determined to make one last appeal directly to the queen. The agents of this movement were the royal treasurer, Luis de Santangel, and Alonzo de Quintanilla. Santangel was the one who presented the cause. On two points he placed special stress, and he urged them with great power and eloquence. The first may be condensed into the phrase that while the loss would, in any event, be but trifling, the gain, in case of success, would be incalculable. In the second place he urged that if the enterprise were not undertaken by Spain, it would doubtless be taken up by one of the rival nations and carried to triumphant success. He then appealed to what the queen was in the habit of doing for the glory of God, the exaltation of the Church, and the extension of her own power and dominion. Here, it was urged, was an opportunity to surpass them all. He called attention to the offer of Columbus to bear an eighth of the expense, and advised her that the requisites for the enterprise would not exceed three thousand crowns. The Marchioness de Moya was present, and added her eloquence to that of Santangel.

These representations had the desired effect, and the queen resolved on the spot to undertake the enterprise. The story, so often repeated, that the queen pledged her jewels for the necessary expense, rests upon no contemporaneous evidence, and has recently been shown to be extremely improbable. It was not necessary, for Santangel declared that he was ready to supply the money out of the treasury of Aragon. The adoption of the cause by the queen was complete and unconditional.

It was in the narrow pass at the foot of Mount Elvira, a few miles from Granada, that the swift messenger of this good news overtook Columbus on his dejected retreat. No very fertile fancy is required to imagine with some confidence the emotions of the explorer as he listened to the story of the queen's new decision. Turning the rein, he hastened his jaded mule with all possible speed to the royal court at Santa Fé.

For reasons which it is not easy to understand, there were still considerable delays before the requisite papers received their final signature. Whether there were disagreements still to be adjusted cannot now be known. Columbus returned to the court early in February, but it was not until the 17th of April that the stipulations had been duly made out and signed.

In form the papers were the work of the royal secretary, but they received the assent and signature of both monarchs. The principal commission is of so much importance that it is here given in full : —

1. First, your Highnesses, in virtue of your dominion over the said seas, shall constitute from this time forth the said Don Christopher Columbus your admiral in all the islands and territories which he may discover or acquire in the said seas, this power to continue in him during his life, and at his death to descend to his heirs and successors from one to another perpetually, with all the dignities and prerogatives appertaining to the said office, and according to the manner in which this dignity has been held by Don Alonzo Henriquez, your High Admiral of Castile, and by the other admirals in their several districts.

2. Furthermore, your Highnesses shall constitute the said Don Christopher Columbus your viceroy and governor-general in all the said islands and territories to be discovered in the said seas ; and for the government of each place three persons shall be named by him, out of which number your Highnesses shall select one to hold the office in question.

3. Furthermore, in the acquisition by trade, discovery, or any other method, of all goods, merchandise, pearls precious stones, gold, silver, spices, and all other articles, within the limits of the said admiralty, the tenth part of their value shall be the property of the said Don Christopher Columbus, after deducting the amount expended

in obtaining them, and the other nine tenths shall be the property of your Highnesses.

4. Furthermore, if any controversy or law-suit should arise in these territories relating to the goods which he may obtain there, or relating to any goods which others may obtain by trade in the same places, the jurisdiction in the said cases shall, by virtue of his office of admiral, pertain to him alone or his deputy, provided the said prerogative belong to the office of admiral, according as that dignity has been held by the above-mentioned Admiral Don Alonzo Henriquez, and the others of that rank in their several districts, and provided the said regulation be just.

5. Furthermore, in the fitting out of any fleets for the purpose of trade in the said territories, the said Don Christopher Columbus shall on every such occasion be allowed the privilege of furnishing one eighth of the expenses of the expedition, and shall at such times receive an eighth part of the profits arising therefrom."

In the formal commission we find these words:

"We therefore by this commission confer on you the office of admiral, viceroy, and governor, to be held in hereditary possession forever, with all the privileges and salaries pertaining thereto."

Surely these were extraordinary powers. From any unjust exercise of supreme authority in the lands Columbus might discover, there was to be no appeal. The authority was limited, moreover, by neither custom nor method. In the matter of governorships he was to have the sole right of nomination, and in all questions of dispute in regard to his own interest in goods obtained either by himself or by anybody else, he or his deputy was to have sole jurisdiction.

The temptation to exercise these powers for the oppression of a barbarous people would seem, even under the most favourable circumstances, to be quite as much as human nature could bear. But the circumstances were not favourable. The danger was in the fact that a high pecuniary premium was put upon the abuse of authority.

The promise of a tenth of all that the Admiral might acquire by trade, discovery, " or any other method," was a powerful stimulant to cruelty and cupidity. Unfortunately, the age was one when every people that did not avow Christianity was regarded as legitimate spoil for the Christian invader. This fact took away the last feeble guarantee of public opinion. In estimating the character of Columbus we must remember that he was subjected to the temptations of unlimited authority, of immeasurable opportunity, and of exemption from all accountability, either to the Government or to public opinion. His place in history must ultimately be determined by the manner in which it shall be shown that he administered this trust.

The fact should not be overlooked that there was always a powerful religious motive in all the plans of Columbus. One of his purposes in seeking to reach eastern Asia by sailing westward was an opening of the way for the conversion of the people to Christianity. His writings abound in expressions of this desire. In all his plans for his expedition he made prominent his wish to gain the means necessary for the conquest of the Holy Land. In his nature and his faith there was much of the religious zeal of the mediæval Crusader, united with a tendency to indulge in the fervid religious rhetoric of the seventeenth-century Puritan. Columbus hoped, by these explorations in the west, to acquire the means of succeeding in that enterprise of bringing Jerusalem back into the control of Christianity, which for three centuries had baffled the efforts of all Christendom.

During the six long years of Columbus's waiting in Spain, the relations of Ferdinand and Isabella to the projects of Columbus were such as to merit our high commendation. We have seen that immediately after his cause was presented to the sovereigns for consideration, it was referred to the most learned men in the vicinity of the court. It is difficult to conjecture how any disposition of the question could, at that time, have been more appropriate. Whenever the subject was presented anew, a similar reference of the subject was made. From no one of these references was there received a favourable report. But when the war had been brought to a close, and when, in consequence, there was opportunity for a personal examination of the matter, the whole subject was taken into sympathetic consideration. The romantic and religious elements of the project appealed strongly to Isabella. Ferdinand acted with characteristic caution. The needed money appears to have been taken from the chest of the king, but only on condition that in due time it should be restored, if need be, from the chest of the queen. Thus it may be said that the husband loaned the trifling subsidy ne-

cessary for the enterprise, on the security of his wife.
This arrangement suited both monarchs, and therefore
both signed the commissions of the Admiral.

If we were asked for the names of those who rendered the highest service to Columbus during this trying period, the answer would not be easy. In the
immediate vicinity of the court Alfonso de Quintanilla was the first to espouse his cause with ardour, and
he remained an unswerving advocate. Among those
to whom the cause was submitted for advice, the
ecclesiastic, Diego de Deza, is entitled to the credit
of having been the first and the most faithful of supporters. The Duke of Medina Celi gave to the navigator the support which detained him at a moment
when he seemed to be on the point of abandoning
Spain forever. The friar of La Rabida, Juan Parez
de Marchena, the old confessor of the queen, made a
successful effort to renew the suit after all hope had
been abandoned. And finally, when the demands of
Columbus seemed preposterous for their magnitude,
the united efforts of Santangel, the Marchioness de
Moya, Quintanilla, and Talavera succeeded in bringing the queen up to the point of a favourable decision.
To all of these advocates no small quota of the credit
for success is due. But in distributing this credit
there must be no forgetting or obscuring of the work
of Columbus himself. We have seen that the advo-
cacy of the navigator was full of inconsistencies and
extravagances. He was a foreigner, and one that
looked very much like an adventurer. The time and
the circumstances seemed the most inopportune. All

these facts argued strongly against his cause. But in spite of them all, his knowledge, his courage, his faith, his tact, and his persistency were enough to hold a band of powerful advocates firmly to his great cause, and, in the end, bring it to success. Whatever abatements from an unreasonable glorification of Columbus modern research may feel compelled to make, these are great qualities, which the progress of time can never efface or obscure.

CHAPTER III.

THE FIRST VOYAGE.

THE commission of Columbus bore date of April 30, 1492. On the same day was signed a royal requisition on the inhabitants of the town of Palos, requiring them to furnish at their own expense two caravels for the expedition. This singular proceeding was in consequence of some offence which the town had given the king and queen, for which the people had been condemned to render the service of two vessels for the period of twelve months, whenever the royal pleasure should call for them. The vessels moreover were to be armed at the expense of the town. Within ten days from the sight of the letter the authorities were required to have the two vessels in complete readiness for the enterprise. The royal treasury was also further relieved by the fact that they were required to furnish the money for the wages of the crew during a period of four months.

Another royal order bearing the same date was of greater importance in its influence on the character of the expedition. All the magistrates in the realm were informed that "every person belonging to the crews of the fleet of said Christopher Columbus" were "exempt from all hindrance or incommodity either in their persons or goods;" and that they were "privi- leged from arrest or detention on account of any offence or crime which may have been committed by them up to the date of this instrument, and during the time they may be on the voyage, and for two months after their return to their homes."

This remarkable order must have been inspired by the fear that the requisite crews for the vessels could not readily be obtained. The special inducements held out to the criminal classes appealed to every debtor, to every defaulter, and to every criminal. Here was immunity from the pursuit of justice. Such an order could hardly have failed to have a powerful influence on the character of the crew. The fleet be- came a refuge for runaway criminals and debtors; and accordingly it was not singular that sailors of respecta- bility were slow to enlist. Popular opinion at Palos was violently opposed to the expedition. Though the town was required to furnish two caravels within ten days after receiving the royal order, weeks passed be- fore the necessary vessels could be procured. A third ship was provided for out of the funds furnished for the expedition. Every shipowner refused to lend his vessel for the enterprise. Another royal order had to be issued, authorizing Columbus to press the ships and men into the service. Meanwhile the mariners of Palos held aloof, partly in the belief that the proposed expedition was simply the work of a monomaniac, and partly from the fact that the ships had been made a refuge for criminals. But Juan Parez, the friar whose influence had already made itself so powerfully felt, was active in persuading men to embark. The Pinzons, who, it will be remembered, had offered to defray one eighth of the expense, now came forward to aid the enterprise with their money and their personal service. Agreeing to take command of two of the vessels, their wealth and their influence gave a new impulse to the undertaking. But enlistments went forward very slowly; and even after men had been enrolled, the least cause of dissatisfaction induced them to desert. In the putting of the ships in order, the work was so badly done as to justify the suspicion that a deliberate effort was put forth to make them unseaworthy.

Though the sovereigns had supposed that ten days would be time enough to put the fleet in readiness for the voyage, it was with the utmost difficulty that the work was accomplished in ten weeks. Columbus had chosen small vessels of less than a hundred tons' burden each, believing that they would be better adapted for service along the coast and in the rivers. It has been estimated that even the longest of them was only sixty-five feet in length, and not more than twenty feet in breadth. The "Santa Maria," commanded by the Admiral himself, was the only one that was decked midships. The others, the "Pinta" and the "Nina," were built high in the prow and stern, that they might the more easily mount the waves, and were covered only at the ends. The "Pinta" was commanded by Columbus's old friend Martin Alonzo Pinzon, while his brother, Vincente Yañez Pinzon, was captain of the "Nina." On all the ships there were a hundred and twenty souls, ninety of them being mariners.

Harrisse has computed the sum provided for the expedition at 1,640,000 maravedis, or about $3640. Of this amount Santangel, as the agent of the monarchs, furnished 1,140,000 maravedis, while Columbus, aided by the Pinzons, provided the remaining five hundred thousand. The fleet's contingent contained a notary for drawing up necessary papers, and a historiographer to put the story in formal order. There was an interpreter learned in all Asiatic tongues, and a metallurgist to examine the ores. Though the fleet was equipped with a physician and a surgeon, it does not appear that it had a priest. The squadron was at length ready to put to sea. We are told that on the last days before sailing, everybody in Palos was impressed with the solemnity of the undertaking. Officers and crew united in going to the church in the most formal manner and confessing themselves, and after partaking of the sacrament, in committing themselves to the special guidance and protection of Heaven. It was an hour before sunrise, on Friday, the 3d of August, when the ships were cut from their moorings and entered upon their perilous adventure.

Fortunately we are not without Columbus's own account of this voyage. The Admiral kept a diary, which, though it is not now known to be in existence, was carefully epitomized by Las Casas, and the abstract, very largely in Columbus's own words, is preserved. There are also still in existence the two

letters of Columbus by means of which the great discovery was formally announced to the world.   It is to
these three priceless documents that we are chiefly
indebted for our knowledge of the voyage.   In the
introduction to the diary Columbus says : " I determined to keep an account of the voyage, and to write
down punctually everything we performed or saw from
day to day."   He also adds : " Moreover, besides
describing every night the occurrences of the day,
and every day those of the preceding night, I intend
to draw up a nautical chart which shall contain the
several parts of the ocean and land in their proper
situations ; and also to compose a book to represent
the whole by pictures, with latitudes and longitudes,
on all which accounts it behooves me to abstain from
sleep and make many efforts in navigation, which
things will demand much labour."

The contemplated geographical work was never
written ; but the purpose of the navigator is of interest, as it creates a presumption in favor of carefulness
in the preparation of the diary.

The general course of the fleet was in a southwesterly direction, the purpose being to touch at the
Canary Islands.   This intention was fortunate ; for on
Monday, the fourth day out, the rudder of the " Pinta "
become loose, and threatened to make a continuance
of the voyage with this vessel impossible.   The Admiral suspected that the accident happened with the
connivance of disaffected members of the crew. Many
of the men had shown an uncompromising opposition
to the expedition before setting out, and there could

be no doubt that any accident that would interrupt the voyage would be most welcome. The " Pinta," however, was in command of Martin Alonzo Pinzon, an officer of capacity and courage, to whose faith in the enterprise Columbus had already been largely indebted while fitting out the fleet and securing the crew. The skill and vigour of the commander caused the rudder to be put in place; but it was again unshipped on the following day, and it was necessary to put into port for repairs.

Owing to delays occasioned by the condition of the " Pinta," it was not until the 12th of August that the little fleet reached port in one of the Canary Islands. Here it was found that the condition of the disabled caravel was worse than had been supposed. Besides having her rudder out of order, she was leaky, and the form of her sails seemed not to be adapted to the perils of an Atlantic voyage. Columbus tried to find another vessel for which he could effect an exchange; however, he was not successful, and so it was found necessary to delay the voyage until the little ship could be put into seaworthy condition. The rudder was made secure, the form of the sails was changed, and every practicable precaution was taken to prevent leakage. But it was not until the 6th of September — more than a month from the day of leaving the port at Palos — that the fleet was once more ready to sail.

During the stay at the Canaries two or three interesting things happened. Columbus reports that they " saw a great eruption of flames from the Peak of Teneriffe, which is a lofty mountain." But more important to the matter in hand were the several reports he heard in regard to the existence of land in the west. The Admiral says he " was assured by many respectable Spaniards inhabiting the island of Ferro that they every year saw land to the west of the Canaries," and also that " others of Gomera affirmed the same with the like assurances." He also makes note of the fact that when he was " in Portugal in 1484 there came a person to the king from the island of Madeira soliciting a vessel to go in quest of land, which he affirmed he saw every year, and always of the same appearance." Still further he says that " he remembers the same was said by the inhabitants of the Azores, and described as in a similar direction, and of the same shape and size."

This interesting delusion, which is supposed to have had its origin in certain meteoric appearances, had taken a firm hold of the credulity of the people. The country which they imagined they saw in the west bore the name of the isle of Brandon, in commemoration of Saint Brandon, a Benedictine monk of the sixth century, who, it was believed, spent seven years in the region to which his name was finally given. Belief in the existence of land not very far west of the Canary group was current in the fifteenth century, and several expeditions were undertaken, by order of the king of Portugal, for the discovery of this mystical continent. As yet, however, the repeated failures of these efforts had not convinced the inhabitants of the islands west of Africa that land within any possible range of vision from the Canaries had no existence except in the imaginations of the beholders. The special connection of this credulity with the expedition of Columbus is in the influence which it must have had upon the spirits of the crew. While there was an air of mystery about it that may have been depressing to certain temperaments, to the mass of the crew it can hardly have failed to give some encouragement. But at the same time it undoubtedly provided the way for a depressing reaction when, after days of fruitless sailing, no land was discovered.

On the morning of the 6th of September the little fleet put out from the harbour of Gomera and entered again upon its course. A report was brought by a vessel from the neighbouring island of Ferro that there were three Portuguese caravels cruising in search of Columbus. This circumstance was interpreted to mean a hostile intent on the part of the king of Portugal, owing to the fact that the Admiral had abandoned his service and resorted to the patronage of Spain. But if the report was true, the Spanish squadron was successful in evading its enemies. The course now taken was due west; but owing to a strong head-sea, progress for several days was very slow.

We have already had occasion to see that Columbus never attached very great importance to the matter of precision in the statement of fact. The recent scrutiny to which his writings have been subjected has revealed so many contradictions and inac-

6

curacies that we are forced into the belief that he often used words in a very general rather than in a specific and strictly accurate sense. We shall not infrequently have occasion to note this habit of mind, — a peculiarity which it will be necessary to remember if we would form an accurate conclusion as to the value of his testimony. He seems not to have been without conscience; but it is not too much to say that whenever there was a powerful motive for misrepresentation, Columbus did not hesitate to ask himself whether the end would not justify the means. The modern ethical standard, which requires absolute truthfulness at all hazards, did not prevail at the end of the fifteenth century; but it is not without much regret that even at that period we find one whom we would gladly rank as a moral hero admitting frankly that he systematically prevaricated in order to convey a false impression. If, on the one hand, there are those who will succeed in finding adequate excuse for the misrepresentation indulged in, on the other it will be hard to find any one who will regard such misrepresentation as a characteristic of lofty conscientiousness.

In the journal of September 9 we find this entry : —

"Sailed this day nineteen leagues, and determined to count less than the true number, that the crew might not be dismayed if the voyage should prove long."

On the following day Columbus says, —

"This day and night sailed sixty leagues, at the rate of ten miles an hour, which are two leagues and a half.

Reckoned only forty-eight leagues, that the crew might not be terrified if they should be long upon the voyage."

In the days following, similar entries were made, always with the same end in view. Interesting evidences of life were often observed. On the 13th of September one of the crew saw a tropical bird, which, it was believed, never goes farther than twenty-five leagues from land. On the 16th large patches of weed were found which appeared to have been recently washed away from land; on account of which the Admiral writes that "they judged themselves to be near some island;" "the continent," continues the narrator, "we shall find farther ahead." These indications multiplied from day to day. On the 18th the "Pinta," which, notwithstanding her bad condition, was a swift sailer, ran ahead of the other vessels, the captain having informed the Admiral that he had seen large flocks of birds toward the west, and that he expected that night to reach land. Though as yet they had only reached the centre of the Atlantic, on the 19th the ships were visited by two pelicans, — birds which, it was said, were not accustomed to go twenty leagues from land. On the 21st the ocean seemed to be covered with weeds; and the same day a whale was seen, — "an indication of land," says the journal, "as whales always keep near the coast." The next day a wind sprang up, whereupon the Admiral observes: "This head-wind was very necessary to me, for my crew had grown much alarmed, dreading that they never should meet in these seas with a fair wind to return to Spain."

On September 25 the disappointing monotony of these indications was interrupted. At sunset Pinzon called out from his vessel that he saw land. The Admiral says, when he heard him declare this, he fell down on his knees and returned thanks to God. Pinzon and his crew repeated "Gloria in excelsis Deo," as did the crew of the Admiral. Those on board the "Nina" ascended the rigging, and all declared that they saw land. The Admiral judged that the land was distant about twenty-five leagues. It was not until the afternoon of the 26th that they discovered that what they had taken for land was nothing but clouds.

As revealed by the journal, the events of each day were much like those of every other. The most striking feature of the voyage was the constantly occurring indications of land. After the little fleet passed mid-ocean there was scarcely a day that did not bring some sign that beckoned them on. Sea-weed abounded, and as a sounding of two hundred fathoms revealed nothing but a steady undercurrent of the ocean, the weeds could not have come from the bottom of the sea. At one time a green rush was found, which, the commanders thought, must have grown in the open air, with its roots in the soil. At another, a piece of wood was taken aboard that gave unmistakable signs of having been somewhat curiously wrought by the hand of man. But the most significant tokens were the birds. They appeared in considerable numbers almost, if not quite, every day, many of them known to be unaccustomed to wan-

der for any very great distance from land. To
every thinking man on board the squadron they
seemed to give evidence absolutely unmistakable that
they were not far from land, and that the object of
their expedition was likely to be successful. The
birds, moreover, so far as any general direction of
their flying could be regarded as an indication,
seemed to have their home in a southwesterly
direction. This fact led the commander of the
" Pinta " to urge the Admiral to change his course.
At first Columbus thought it best, in spite of the
course of the birds, to keep on due west. But at
length the indications were so unmistakable and so
persistent that he yielded, and set the rudders for a
southwesterly course. But for this incident, seemingly very trifling in itself, the fleet, as Humboldt
has remarked, would have entered the Gulf Stream
before touching land, and would have been borne to
a landfall somewhere on the coast of the future
United States.

Many of the later historians of Columbus, taking
the hint from Oviedo, have given graphic pictures
of the way in which the skill and the tact of the
Admiral prevented the crew of the fleet from breaking
out into mutinous revolt and turning the vessels
toward home. It has been said that at one time
there was a serious purpose of throwing the Admiral
into the sea, and declaring that he fell overboard
while making an observation ; at another, that Columbus found himself compelled to promise that unless
land was discovered within three days, he would

abandon the expedition, turn about, and sail for home. But these stories must now, for the most part, be regarded as apocryphal. None of them are mentioned by Columbus himself, nor do they appear in the other early accounts of the voyage. No hint of mutiny or even of any lack of due subordination appears in the searching trials of 1513 and 1515, when every event that could possibly have a bearing upon the methods of Columbus was brought upon the witness-stand. As a matter of fact, the voyage was for the most part an uneventful one, save as its placid progress was occasionally excited by the variations of the compass, an unusual amount of sea-weed, or an unwonted flight of birds. That the hopes and fears of the crews were alert cannot of course be doubted, but there is no evidence sufficient to justify the belief that the life of the Admiral or the advance of the expedition was ever in serious danger.

In the evening of the 11th of October, Columbus thought that he discovered a light moving with fitful gleams in the darkness. He called to him two of his companions, one of whom confirmed his impression, while the other could not. The journal says that "The Admiral again perceived it once or twice, appearing like the light of a candle moving up and down, which some thought an indication of land." But evidently Columbus did not regard this as a discovery, for he not only reminded the crew of the reward of a pension that awaited the one who should first see land, but he also offered a silk doublet as an additional inducement to the search. They were still some forty-two miles from the coast, which lies so low that it could hardly have been seen at a distance of twenty. It was four hours later that land was first unmistakably seen in the moonlight, at a distance of about two leagues. There can be no question that if a light was really seen at all, it was on a boat at some distance from the shore. A reward of ten thousand maravedis per year had been promised by the king and queen to the person on the expedition who should first descry land. Columbus in his journal admits that land was first seen and announced by Rodrigo de Triana of the " Pinta " at two o'clock on the morning of October 12th; and it would be a pleasure to record that he subsequently had sufficient magnanimity to waive his own very absurd claim in favour of the poor sailor to whom it was so justly due. But after his return he set up the demand for himself; and to him it was promptly adjudged and paid by the king and queen. It is said that the poor sailor, thinking himself ignobly defrauded, renounced Christianity and went to live among the Mohammedans, whom he regarded as a juster people.

It was then on Friday, October 12, that the fleet first came to land upon an island which the natives called Guanahani. Early in the morning Columbus and the brothers Pinzon and the notary entered a boat with the royal standard and made for the shore. The rest of the crews immediately followed. As soon as they had landed, the requisite formalities were performed, and witnesses were summoned to

note that, before all others, Columbus took possession of the island for the king and queen, his sovereigns.   He gave it the name of San Salvador.

Over the question as to the spot where Columbus
first landed there has been much difference of opinion.   The narrative of the Admiral concerning this
important part of his voyage, though it has been preserved entire, is not so free from ambiguities, or so
definite in its positive statements, as to relieve the
subject of doubt.   The reckoning of Columbus, moreover, on the matter of longitude and latitude was
not sufficiently accurate to throw much light on the
subject.   Accordingly, several of the Bahamas have
had their advocates.   The modern San Salvador, or
Cat Island, was believed to be the place of landing
by Humboldt and Irving.   South of Cat Island lie
Watling's, Samana, Acklin, and the Grand Turk ; and
no one of them has been without its ardent supporters.   Recently, however, the most careful students
of the problem have unmistakably drifted toward
the belief that the spot of the landfall should be confidently fixed upon Watling's Island.

The arguments in favour of this locality were first
elaborately set forth by Captain Becher in a volume
published in 1856, and were followed by Peschel two
years later in his " History of Modern Discovery."
Mr. R. H. Major, a careful student of the subject, was
for many years inclined to favour Turk's Island ; but
in 1870 he conceded that the weight of evidence was
in favour of Watling's.   Lieutenant Murdock of the
American navy and Mr. Charles A. Schott of the

United States Coast Survey reached the same conclusion by independent studies in 1884, as did also Mr.
Clements R. Markham in 1889. Finally, and perhaps most important of all, the Bahamas were visited
and this problem was carefully studied in November
of 1890 by the German explorer Herr Rudolf Cronau, with the result of establishing Watling's Island as
the site of the landfall beyond any reasonable doubt.

Cronau's investigations are twofold in their nature :
the first point of his inquiry being devoted to the
reasons for thinking Watling's the island on which
Columbus landed ; the second, to establishing the
point at which the landfall took place. Though
it is on this last point that special significance is to
be attached to his investigations, it may not be out of
place to give a brief summary of the argument as a
whole.

Columbus describes the island as low, covered with
abundant and luxuriant vegetation, and as having a
large body of water in the interior. In one place he
speaks of the island as "small," at another as "pretty
large." After the first landing, he goes N. N. E. in
the small boats, and soon passes through a narrow entrance into a harbour "large enough to accommodate
the fleets of Christendom." In this harbour he dis-
covers an admirable site of a fort, which he describes
with minute care. He says, moreover, that the part of
the island visited is protected by an outlying reef of
rocks not far from the shore. Las Casas, who became very familiar with the islands during the life of
Columbus, and who probably knew where the first

landing was made, states that the form of the island was oblong, or "bean-shaped." The length of Watling's Island is about twelve English miles, the breadth between four and six. All these characteristics apply to Watling's, and in their entirety they apply to no other.

There are, however, certain difficulties in the way of accepting this theory. The most serious is the fact that the rocks off the northern, eastern, and southern parts of the island are so formidable as to offer no safe place for anchorage, and that an approach from none of these directions could afford the view described by Columbus. It is in meeting this difficulty that the ingenious theory of Cronau is of importance. It is in substance as follows.

The journal of Columbus tells us that on Thursday, October 11, the ships "encountered a heavier sea than they had met with before in the whole voyage." It also states that in the course of twenty-four hours they made the remarkable run of fifty-nine leagues, running at times "ten miles an hour, at others twelve, at others seven." In the evening of the 11th, "from sunset till two hours after midnight," the average rate was "twelve miles an hour." It was at ten o'clock that Columbus reports that he saw the light, and consequently the vessel must have advanced forty-eight miles before two o'clock on the morning of the 12th, when land was seen by Triana from the "Pinta." These facts, together with the extraordinary length of the run on the 11th, indicate unmistakably that the roughness of the sea was caused by a strong easterly wind, for by no other means could so rapid an advance have been made. At "two o'clock," says the Admiral, "land was discovered at a distance of two leagues." In which direction the land lay is not indicated. All sails "except the square sail" were taken in, and the vessels "lay to" till day, — probably about four or five hours. The supposition of Cronau is that a wind which up to two o'clock carried them when under full sail twelve miles an hour, must have borne the ships, when under square sail, at least ten or fifteen miles before dawn. It would have been impossible in a heavy sea to land on the rocky coast of the east side ; and whatever the advance, it must have been either on the north or on the south. It seems reasonable to suppose that the fleet found itself at the break of day west of the island. In any case, good seamanship required that they should seek anchorage in a high wind on the lee, or west side ; and accordingly, the only natural course was for them to turn about and approach the island from the west. On the supposition that this course was pursued, no difficulties whatever are found in reconciling Columbus's narrative with the present condition of the island. At about the middle of the west coast the locality at present known as Riding Rocks must have presented then, as it does now, an inviting anchorage. All the features of the coast as described by Columbus are now easily identified. The sail to the N. E. E., which under any other hypothesis presents insurmountable difficulties, is now easily explained. Taking a boat and following along the same course, Cronau entered the mouth of the harbour, and readily distinguished all the characteristics described by the Admiral.

If the data given by Columbus afford no very definite clew to the spot on which the landing took place, his account of what he saw, especially of the people, is so replete with interest as to justify a quotation of some length. After describing the formalities of the taking possession of the island, and noting that the trees seemed very green, that there were many streams of water and divers sorts of fruits, Columbus gives the following graphic account of the natives : —

"As I saw that they were very friendly to us, and perceived that they could be much more easily converted to our holy faith by gentle means than by force, I presented them with some red caps, and strings of beads to wear upon the neck, and many other trifles of small value, wherewith they were much delighted, and became wonderfully attached to us. Afterwards they came swimming to the boats, bringing parrots, balls of cotton thread, javelins, and many other things, which they exchanged for articles we gave them, such as glass beads and hawk's bells, which trade was carried on with the utmost good will. But they seemed on the whole to me to be a very poor people. They all go completely naked, even the women, though I saw but one girl. All whom I saw were young, not above thirty years of age, well made, with fine shapes and faces; their hair short and coarse like that of a horse's tail, combed toward the forehead, except a small portion which they suffer to hang down behind, and never cut. Some paint themselves with black, which makes them appear like those of the Canaries, neither black nor white; others with white, others with red, and

others with such colours as they can find. Some paint
the face, and some the whole body; others only the eyes,
and others the nose. Weapons they have none, nor are
they acquainted with them; for I showed them swords,
which they grasped by the blades, and cut themselves
through ignorance. They have no iron, their javelins
being without it, and nothing more than sticks, though
some have fish-bones or other things at the ends. They
are all of a good size and stature, and handsomely
formed. I saw some with scars of wounds upon their
bodies, and demanded by signs the cause of them. They
answered me in the same way, that there came people
from the other islands in the neighbourhood who endeavoured to make prisoners of them, and they defended
themselves. I thought then, and still believe, that these
were from the continent. It appears to me that the people are ingenious, and would be very good servants; and
I am of the opinion that they would readily become Christians, as they appear to have no religion. They very
quickly learn such words as are spoken to them. If it
please our Lord, I intend at my return to carry home six
of them to your Highnesses, that they may learn our language. I saw no beasts in the island, nor any sort of
animals except parrots."

The next three months of this renowned expedition
were spent in going from island to island, in making
brief visits to the various places that seemed to promise any interesting or important revelation, and in
seeking for objects of interest and value. The Admiral was in constant hope of learning something that
would direct him to Cipango. In all the islands the
people were found to speak the same language and to
have the same general characteristics. After visiting

and exploring Long Island and Saometo, which he respectively named Fernandina and Isabella, he at length, on the 21st day of October, landed on the northern coast of a large island which the natives called Colba. This was the modern Cuba. He explored the picturesque region far to the west, and found it so large that he supposed it to be a continent. The Indians, however, informed him that it was only an island. As he perceived neither towns nor villages near the sea-coast, but only scattered habitations, the people of which fled at his approach, he sent two of his men into the interior to learn whether the inhabitants had either king or chief. The men, after an absence of three days, reported that they found a vast number of settlements built of wood and straw, with "innumerable people." Yet they were able to discover no indications of any kind of government. To the island the name Juana was given, in honor of Don Juan.

Columbus did not attempt to circumnavigate the island. After coasting far to the west, and noting carefully the rivers and harbours, he resolved to retrace his course. From the point where the first landing was made, he sailed a hundred and seven leagues toward the east, when he came to a cape from which he reports that he saw another island, about eighteen leagues away. This was the island now known as San Domingo, or Hayti, to which Columbus gave the name Hispaniola. Sailing thither, and skirting along its northern coast, the explorers found it more beautiful even than any of the others they had seen. The journal describes the harbours as far more safe and commodious than any to be found in Christian countries; the rivers were large and noble, the land was high, with beautiful mountains and lofty ridges covered with a thousand varieties of beautiful trees that "seemed to reach to heaven." Most gratifying of all, they learned from the Indians that there were "large mines of fine gold."

It was here that Columbus decided to establish the first permanent settlement. Through the carelessness of the pilot, however, the Admiral's own vessel struck upon a rock off the northwestern coast of the island, and, finally, in spite of all the efforts of the crew, had gone to pieces. The assistance rendered by the natives in rescuing the stores of the wreck afforded touching evidence of their friendly feeling. The timbers of the ship furnished the material for a structure that should at once be a storehouse and a fort. It was resolved to leave provisions for a year, together with seeds and implements for the cultivation of the soil.

As to the number of the crew that were left at this new settlement, the authorities do not agree. It is probable, however, that there were about forty. In the narrative of Columbus, the words are these: "I have directed that there shall be provided a store of timber for the construction of the fort, with a provision of bread and wine for more than a year, seed for planting, the long boat of the ship, a calker, a carpenter, a gunner, a cooper, and many other persons among the number of those who have earnestly

desired to serve your Highnesses and oblige me by
remaining here, and searching for the gold mine."
As the wreck and the consequent determination to
build a fort and establish a colony occurred on Christmas Day, the Admiral named the new settlement " La
Navidad."

The people of the island manifested a most
friendly disposition. The abode of the king was
about a league and a half distant from the shoal
where the wreck had taken place. Columbus relates
that when the Spanish messengers informed the cacique of the misfortune, he "shed tears and despatched all the people of the town with large canoes
to unload the ship." Again he says that the king,
" with his brothers and relations, came to the shore
and took every care that the goods should be brought
safely to land and carefully preserved. From time
to time, he sent his relations to the Admiral, weeping
and consoling him, and entreating him not to be
afflicted at his loss, for he would give him all he had."
The Admiral still further observes that "in no part of
Castile would more strict care have been taken of the
goods, that the smallest trifle be not lost." And
again: "The king ordered several houses to be
cleared for the purpose of storing the goods." On
the following day, Wednesday, December 26, the
Admiral's journal contains this memorandum: "At
sunrise the king of the country visited the Admiral
on board the 'Nina,' and with tears in his eyes en-
treated him not to indulge in grief, for he would give
him all he had; that he had already assigned the

Spaniards on shore two large houses, and, if necessary, would grant others, and as many canoes as could be used in bringing the goods and crew to land, — which, in fact, he had done the day before, without the smallest trifle being purloined." In forming an opinion of a policy which in a few years completely annihilated the inhabitants of these islands, this estimate of their character ought not to be forgotten.

Before leaving this settlement, Columbus took the precaution to give to the natives an exhibition of the force of fire-arms. A lombard was loaded and fired against the side of the stranded ship. The shot, much to the amazement of the natives, passed through the hull of the vessel, and struck the water on the farther side. He also gave them a representation of a battle fought by parties of the crew, and conducted in accordance with Christian methods. This was done, as he informs us, "to strike terror into the inhabitants and make them friendly to the Spaniards left behind."

Having left the settlement in charge of Diego de Arana, and three others as subordinate officers, and having conferred upon them all the powers he had himself received from the king and queen, Columbus prepared to enter upon his homeward voyage. The commander of the "Pinta," who, as we shall presently see, had entered upon an exploring expedition of his own, had now rejoined the Admiral ; and on the 4th of January the two little ships turned their rudders and set sail for home.

In the study of the journal and the letters of Columbus, in so far as they relate to the first voyage, a number of impressions are strongly, and, it should perhaps be said, painfully, stamped upon the mind of the reader.

While the desire of the explorer to Christianize the island was never lost sight of, he was prevented from any missionary work, not only by the fact that the expedition was unaccompanied by priests, but also by the nature of the expedition itself. It was simply a voyage of discovery; and the movements from one island to another were necessarily too rapid to admit of anything more than a temporary impression. Nothing more, therefore, was done to propagate Christianity than to leave here and there upon the islands the mysterious emblems of the new faith. The preaching of the Gospel was reserved for future expeditions.

But the ultimate Christianizing of the natives was only one of the religious motives that inspired the expedition. For many years Columbus had entertained the hope that gold might be found in quantity sufficient to enable the Spanish Government to rescue the Holy Sepulchre from the possession of infidels. The project inspired him throughout his life. From these, as well as from personal motives, he was therefore particularly desirous of finding gold. Nothing is more painfully obvious in his journal than the power of this pecuniary motive. The quest for gold lured him on from one island to another, and from the sea-coast to the interior. He everywhere makes inquiries for gold, and again and again he hears reports of gold mines ; but his efforts in search of them are always unsuccessful. However, he never abandons hope. The journal abounds in expression of optimistic expectation that gold in vast quantities will yet be found, and that the object of this search will yet be fully realized. But the gold-bearing mines every-where eluded him, and indeed the natives appear to have possessed the precious metal in no more than very trifling quantities. Still, the hopes of Columbus were kept sanguine to the last. It was only ten days before the expedition sailed for home that he entered upon his journal the expression of a most sanguine expectation. Las Casas tells us that in his journal for December 26th, Columbus "adds that he hopes to find on his return from Castile a ton of gold collected by them in trading with the natives, and that they will have succeeded in discovering the mine and the spices, and all these in such abundance that before three years the king and queen may undertake the recovery of the Holy Sepulchre. ' For I have before protested to your Highnesses,' continues Columbus, 'that the profits of this enterprise shall be employed in the conquest of Jerusalem, at which your High-nesses smiled, and said you were pleased, and had the same inclination.' "

In one of the letters of the Admiral announcing the discovery, known as the Sanchez Letter, the Admiral writes in still more sanguine terms. He says : " To sum up the whole, and state briefly the great profits of this voyage, I am able to promise the acquisition, by a trifling assistance from their Majesties, of any quantity of gold, drugs, cotton, and mastick, which last article is found only in the island of Scio; also any quantity of aloe, and as many slaves for the service of the marine as their Majesties may stand in need of."

In the letter written to the royal treasurer, Sant-angel, Columbus invariably speaks in terms of similar confidence. "In conclusion, and to speak only of what I have performed," says he, "this voyage, so hastily despatched, will, as their Highnesses may see, enable any desirable quantity of gold to be obtained, by a very small assistance afforded me on their part." On the eve of sailing for Spain, after referring to the opposition he had received from the clergy and others about the court, he says: "These last have been the cause that the royal crown of your High-nesses does not possess this day a hundred millions of reals more than when I entered your service, from which time it will be seven years the 20th day of this month of January."

The reader will hardly fail to observe that these promises, so comprehensive in their nature, rested upon a very slender foundation. Very little gold had been seen by the explorers, and the mines had all baffled their most diligent search. The ardent nature of Columbus found no difficulty in converting hopes into confident expectations. How painfully these were destined to be disappointed, we shall have occasion hereafter to see.

Another matter that is worthy of notice is the general attitude of Columbus toward his crew and toward the islanders. It may be difficult to deter-

mine how far it was Columbus's fault; but the fact
is unmistakable that there are no indications of any
attachment to him by any of the members of his
crew. His habit of deceiving them in regard to the
distance passed over, and in regard to the needle, is
likely to have occasioned general distrust. Certain
it is that Martin Alonzo Pinzon, the ardent friend
whose support at Palos made the expedition possible,
deserted him without warning soon after the fleet
reached the first land. The Admiral himself says,
in his journal of November 21st, that Pinzon, " in-
cited by cupidity," sailed away with the " Pinta "
" without leave of the Admiral," and that " by
his language and action he occasioned many other
troubles."

But the conduct of Pinzon was even to Columbus
something of a mystery; for elsewhere in his journal
he " confesses himself unable to learn the cause of
the unfavorable disposition which this man had manifested toward him throughout the voyage." Elsewhere the Admiral says Pinzon " was actuated solely
by haughtiness and cupidity in abandoning him."
Again he says that both of the Pinzon brothers " had
a party attached to them, the whole of whom had
displayed great haughtiness and avarice, disobeying
his commands, regardless of the honours he had conferred upon them."

It is evident that Columbus was quite devoid of
tact in the management of men; for the bitterness
that at a later period manifested itself could not
otherwise be accounted for.

Toward the natives Columbus seems not to have been actuated by any motives of cruelty. He is not to be harshly judged, moreover, if his methods were simply those of the fifteenth rather than those of the nineteenth century. But human nature is ever essentially the same, and it is therefore easy to understand the history of the change that rapidly came over the spirit of the natives. Immediately after he arrived at the islands, Columbus took a number of the natives by force, and kept them upon the ship. On the 12th day of November he writes: "Yesterday a canoe came to the ship with six young men; five of them came on board, whom I ordered to be detained, in order to have them with me. I then sent ashore to one of the houses and took seven women and three children; this I did that the Indians might tolerate their captivity better with their company." In the same connection the Admiral adds: "These women will be of great help to us in acquiring their language, which is the same throughout all these countries, the inhabitants keeping up a communication among the islands by means of their canoes." Again, on the 14th of January, only two days before taking final leave, Las Casas says that, "wishing to make prisoners of some Indians, he intended to despatch a boat in the night to visit their houses for this purpose; but the wind blowing strong from the east and northeast occasioned a rough sea, which prevented it." On the following day he says: "There came four young Indians on board the caravel, where they gave so good an account to the Admiral of the

island to the east that he determined to take them
along with him."

It is impossible to reflect upon this habit of the
Admiral without realizing that, however friendly
and hospitable the natives had shown themselves at
first, the impression soon made upon their minds
must have been one of the utmost repugnance and
enmity. To indulge in any other supposition would
be to suppose that the natives were not human beings. The captives seem for the most part to have
been kindly treated, and they may not have manifested an unconquerable aversion to their captivity;
but this unscrupulous policy of kidnapping the natives whenever opportunity offered, could not have
been otherwise than disastrous to all friendly relations. It is impossible to conceive that the islanders
were so devoid of all human sensibilities as to see
with indifference their husbands and wives, their sons
and daughters, stolen from them for the gratification
of the lust and the cupidity of their visitors. Nor,
aside from all moral considerations, on the part of
the wisest historian of the time was there any failure
to understand the disastrous consequences of such
a policy. Las Casas was fully alive to all the political significance of this course of action. While this
great moralist, whose nobility of character raises him
far above all the other public men of his time, fully
acquits Columbus of any wrong intent, he does not
hesitate to indict him for initiating a policy that was
the cause of all the crimes and disasters that ensued.
The right to kidnap was of course resented by the

natives. The consequence was a war of extermination. The sad fate of the colony of La Navidad can never be fully understood, for reasons which in due time we shall see ; but it would have been strange indeed if men, endowed with even the feeblest attributes of human nature, had not been desirous of exterminating a race actuated by such a policy. The words of Las Casas are at once so judicious and so just that they ought not to be abridged. After speaking of the ardent desire of Columbus to bring as much profit as possible to Ferdinand and Isabella, he uses these admirable words : —

"For this cause the Admiral thought and watched and worked for nothing more than to contrive that there might come advantage and income to the sovereigns. . . . Ignoring that which ought not to be ignored concerning divine and natural right and the right judgment of reason, he introduced and commenced to establish such principles and to sow such seeds that there originated and grew from them such a deadly and pestilential herb, and one which produced such deep roots, that it has been sufficient to destroy and devastate all these Indies, without human power sufficing to impede or intercept such great and irreparable evils."

And then, with a charming discrimination and charity, the same benignant author continues, —

"I do not doubt that if the Admiral had believed there would succeed such pernicious detriment as did succeed, and had known as much of the primary and secondary conclusions of natural and divine right as he knew of cosmography and other human doctrines, he would never have dared to introduce or establish a thing which was to produce such calamitous evils; for no one can say that he was not a good and Christian man."

The course taken by Columbus does not show that he was exceptionally immoral; for morality is at least so conventional as to be entitled to be judged in the light of the age under consideration. But his course does show that he was not above the moral debasement of the age in which he lived, on the one hand, and, on the other, that he was destitute, not only of the characteristics of what we call statesmanship, but also of ordinary tact and good judgment. Nothing could have been easier than by a judicious use of rewards and inducements to persuade a sufficient number of the natives to accompany the fleet in a most friendly spirit. Either this was not perceived, or it was not desired. In either case, the whole history is a sad commentary on the management of the Admiral.

In spite of the popular superstition, Columbus did not hesitate to set sail for home on Friday. It had been on Friday that he left Palos; on Friday that he left the Canaries; and now on Friday, the 4th of January, he took leave of the colony at La Navidad and ordered the pilots to set the rudder for home. On the 9th day of January they proceeded thirty-six leagues, as far as Punta Roxa, or Red Point, where the Admiral records that they found tortoises as big as bucklers, and where also he saw three mermaids that raised themselves far above the water. Of the latter the Admiral has the frankness to say that although they had something like a human face, they were not so handsome as they are painted. Two days later Columbus came to a mountain covered with snow, which he named Monte de Plata ; and, a little beyond, after passing a succession of capes, which were duly named, he came to a vast bay in which he determined to remain to observe the conjunction that was to be seen on the 17th. Here for the first time he found men with bows and arrows, and not only bought a bow and some arrows, but learned from one of the natives that the Caribs were to the eastward, and that gold was to be found on an island not far away, which he called the island of St. John. Bernaldez says that "in the islands of these Caribs, as well as in the neighbouring ones, there is gold in incalculable quantity, cotton in vast abundance, and especially spices, such as pepper, which is four times as strong and pungent as the pepper that we use in Spain."

It soon became evident that these people were of a less pacific nature than the other islanders whom Columbus had met. A band of fifty-five of the natives, armed with bows and arrows and swords of hard wood, as well as heavy spears, attempted to seize seven of the Spaniards. An altercation ensued. Two of the Indians were wounded, whereupon they all fled, leaving their arms behind them. The incident is worthy of note from the fact that it was the only time during this expedition that the Spaniards and the natives came to blows. The breach was easily healed, however, for on the following day the

Indians returned as though nothing had happened, and a complete reconciliation took place. The Admiral gave the native king a red cap, and the next day "the king sent his gold crown and provisions."

On the 15th, Columbus entered the port of a little island where there were good salt pits. The soil, the woods, and the plains convinced him that at last he had come to the island of Cipango. Perhaps he was confirmed in this impression by the current reports that the gold mines of Cibao were not far distant. On the next day the Spaniards discovered the caravel "Pinta" sailing toward them. Twenty days before, Pinzon, apparently moved by a resistless ambition, had gone off on an independent cruise. Columbus now received the excuse of the captain, — that he acted under necessity; and though he thought it by no means satisfactory, he was willing to condone the offence.

The Admiral now decided to sail directly for Spain; and accordingly the Spaniards prepared at once to leave the bay, which they called De las Flechas, or the Bay of Arrows. When they had advanced about sixteen leagues, the Indians pointed to the island of St. John, which, they said, was the home of the Caribs, or cannibals. Columbus did not think it wise, however, to delay for further investigation or inquiry. Sails were set, and the prows of the two little ships were turned toward home. It was on the 16th of January that the last of the Bahamas passed to the rearward out of sight.

During several days the navigators had no adverse

fortune. The killing of a tunny-fish and a shark afforded a welcome addition to their larder, as they were
now reduced to bread and wine. The "Pinta" soon
proved to be in poor condition for the voyage, as
her mizzen-mast was out of order and could carry
but little sail. The sea was calm and the course was
east by northeast until February 4, when it was
changed to east. On the 10th the pilots and the
captains took observations to determine their bear-
ings, but with very unsatisfactory results. The imperfect condition of the science of navigation was
well illustrated by the fact that their reckonings
differed by a hundred and fifty leagues.

The calm monotony of the voyage was broken on
the 13th. All night they laboured with a high wind
and furious sea. On the next day the storm increased,
"the waves crossing and dashing against one another,
so that the vessel was overwhelmed." In the following night the two little ships made signals by lights
as long as one could see the other. At sunrise the
wind increased, and the sea became more and more
terrible. The "Pinta" was nowhere to be seen, and
the Admiral thought her lost. The journal records
that he ordered lots to be cast for one of them to go
on a pilgrimage to St. Mary of Guadaloupe, and
carry a wax taper of five pounds weight, and that he
caused them all to take oath that the one on whom
the lot fell should make the pilgrimage. For this
purpose as many peas were put into a hat as there
were persons on board, one of the peas being marked
with a cross. The first person to put his hand in the

hat was the Admiral, and he drew the crossed pea.
Two other lots were taken, one of these also falling
to Columbus. They then made a vow to go in procession in penitential garments to the first church
dedicated to Our Lady which they might meet with
on arriving at land, and there pay their devotions.

But notwithstanding these vows the danger continued to increase. Lack of ballast was partially
supplied by filling with sea-water such casks as they
could make available. It is easy to conjecture what
the anxiety of the Admiral must have been. One
of the vessels had been lost in the Indies; the
"Pinta" had also probably perished; and now the
fury of the hurricane was such as to make it extremely
improbable that even the "Nina" would survive. In
such a calamitous event no word of the discovery
would ever reach Europe, and all the worst conjectures of the opponents of the expedition would seem
to have been fulfilled.

As a possible means of preventing so disastrous a
result, Columbus wrote upon parchment an account
of the voyage and of the discoveries he had made,
and after rolling it up in waxed cloth, well tied,
and putting it into a large wooden cask, he threw it
into the sea. Another he placed upon the deck of
the vessel, in order that in case all upon the vessel
should be lost, there might be a chance that the
results of the voyage might still be made known.

At sunrise of the 15th, land was discovered, which
some thought to be Madeira, and others the rock
of Cintra, near Lisbon. According to the Admiral's

reckoning, however, they were nearer the Azores. But the power of the storm was still so great that it was not until the morning of the 18th that they were able to come to an anchorage, and to find that they were in the group of the Azores, at the island of St. Mary.

Columbus now sent a half of the crew on shore to fulfil their vows, intending on their return to go himself with the other half, for the same purpose. But the first company of pilgrims were set upon by the Portuguese and taken prisoners. An attempt, though unsuccessful, was also made to capture the Admiral. A severe altercation occurred, in which the captain of the island ordered the Admiral on shore, and the Admiral in turn displayed his commission and threatened the island with devastation. It was not until the 22d that the parleyings came to an end and the captured portion of the crew was restored.

Though for a few days the weather was propitious, on the 27th another storm came on, which continued for several days. On the 3d day of March a violent squall struck the vessel and split all the sails. They were again in such imminent danger that another pilgrimage was promised, and the crew all made a vow to fast on bread and water on the first Saturday after their landing. Having lost its sails, the vessel was now driven under bare poles before the wind. Through the night Columbus says that the "Nina" was kept afloat "with infinite labor and apprehension." But at the dawn of the 4th of March the Spaniards found they were off the rock of Cintra.

Though from what had occurred, the Admiral entertained a strong distrust of the Portuguese Government,
there was no alternative but to run into the port for
shelter.

In view of his experience during the returning voyage, Columbus can hardly have been surprised to
learn from some of the oldest mariners of the place
that so tempestuous a winter had never been known.
He received numerous congratulations on what was
regarded as a miraculous preservation.

Immediately on reaching the port the Admiral made
formal announcement of his discoveries. A courier
was despatched to the king and queen of Spain with
the tidings. To the king of Portugal a letter was
also sent requesting permission and authority to land
at Lisbon, as a report that his vessel was laden with
treasure had spread abroad and gave him a feeling of
insecurity at the mouth of the Tagus, where he was
surrounded by needy and unscrupulous adventurers.
Accompanying this request was the assurance that the
vessel had not visited any of the Portuguese colonies,
but had come from Cipango and India, which he had
discovered in the course of his westward voyage.

For some days after his arrival Columbus seemed
to be in some danger. For nearly a century Lisbon
had derived its highest glory from maritime discovery,
and it was therefore not singular that the advent of a
vessel with such tidings should have filled the people
with wonder and surprise. From morning till night
the little ship was thronged with visitors piqued with
curiosity. On the day after his arrival, the captain of

a large Portuguese man-of-war summoned Columbus
on board his ship to give an account of himself and
his voyage. The explorer replied that he held a commission as admiral from the sovereigns of Spain, and,
as such, he must refuse to leave his vessel, or to send
any one in his place. This attitude of lofty dignity
was successful. The Portuguese commander visited
the caravel with sound of drums and trumpets, and
made the most generous offers of protection and
service.

On the 8th of March Columbus received an invitation to visit the king at Valparaiso. Complying with
this invitation, he received a friendly greeting. King
John did not scruple to say that in his opinion,
according to the articles stipulated with the Spanish
monarchs, the new discovery belonged to him rather
than to Castile.

This claim was not without some show of reason.
In the time of the Crusades the doctrine had been
promulgated and generally accepted that Christian
princes had a right to invade and seize upon the territories of infidels under the plea of defeating the
enemies of Christ and of extending the sway of the
Church. What particular Christian monarch was to
have the right to a given territory was to be determined by papal decision. Under this authority Pope
Martin V. conceded to the Crown of Portugal all the
lands that might be discovered between Cape Bojador
and the Indies. This concession was formally consented to and ratified by Spain and Portugal in the
treaty of 1479. Though it was evident that the in-

tent of the treaty only related to such lands as might
be discovered in a passage to the Indies by an easterly course, there was no verbal limitation, and
therefore it can hardly be regarded as singular that
the Portuguese monarch should now claim that it
included within its provisions any lands that might be
discovered in even a westerly voyage.

But it is evident that Columbus regarded this question as one to be determined by the monarchs themselves rather than by any discussion between his
royal host and himself. Accordingly, he was content
merely to observe that he had not been aware of the
agreement to which allusion had been made, and
that when setting out on his voyage, he had received
explicit instructions not to interfere with any of the
Portuguese settlements.

Perhaps the only importance to be attached to this
visit to the Portuguese port is the fact that by it Columbus was made fully aware that the king of Portugal intended to contest the rights of Spain to the
newly discovered lands. The claim of the king was
eagerly taken up and seconded by his courtiers, some
of whom were the very men who, ten years before,
had advised against giving Columbus the assistance
he needed, and consequently were piqued at the success that had finally crowned his efforts. They assured
the monarch that the new lands, even if they were
not the identical ones that had been reached by the
Portuguese navigators who had sailed toward the east,
were at least so near them as to make an independent
title invalid. From one absurdity they went on to

another, until they reached the conclusion that the claims of the discoverer were absurd and preposterous, and that they were entitled to no consideration whatever. Spanish and Portuguese historians agree that the king's advisers even went so far as to propose the assassination of the Admiral, in order to prevent any future complications.

It is to the credit of the monarch that, notwithstanding these ignoble proposals of his ministers, he treated Columbus with distinguished personal consideration. The hospitality extended was scarcely less than princely, and on the departure of the navigator the king gave him a royal escort that was commanded to show him every kindness. On his way back to Lisbon the Admiral accepted an invitation to visit the queen at the monastery of Villa Franca, where he regaled her with a glowing and circumstantial account of the expedition and the islands he had discovered.

It must not be supposed, however, that the king was ingenuous. On the contrary, he listened with favour to some of the more subtle and sinister suggestions of his courtiers. The proposal that met with most countenance was the advice that they should fit out a strong fleet at once, and despatch it under command of one of the foremost captains of the Portuguese service, to take possession of the newly discovered country before a second Spanish expedition could reach its destination.

After thus passing nine days within the domain of Portugal, Columbus hoisted anchor on the 13th of

March, and reached the port of Palos on Friday, the 15th, where he was received with great demonstrations of joy.

By the people of this little Spanish port the expedition had been regarded as chimerical and desperate. But the crews had formed no very small portion of the able-bodied men of the town. Many, therefore, had given up their friends as abandoned to the mysterious horrors with which credulity had always peopled the unknown seas. But now, many of their friends had not only returned, but they brought back accounts of the discovery of a new world. The bells were rung, the shops were closed, business of all kinds was suspended, a solemn procession was formed, and wherever Columbus was observed, he was hailed with acclamations.

The court was at Barcelona. The Admiral at once despatched a letter to the king and queen, announcing his arrival, and informing them that he would await their orders at Seville. Before he departed from Palos, however, an event of great interest occurred. On the very evening of the arrival of Columbus, and while the bells of triumph were still ringing, the "Pinta," commanded by Martin Alonzo Pinzon, entered the river. The two little vessels had parted company in the terrible storm off the Azores; and each, supposing that the other was lost, by a singular coincidence now, on the same day, reached the port from which they had together set out more than six months before.

The connection of Martin Alonzo Pinzon with the

first voyage of Columbus is a subject which has received more or less of the attention of every historian of that remarkable event. Unfortunately, the ending of his career was one that threw an indelible stain upon the credit of his name. The concluding facts of his life may be briefly stated. After parting from the " Nina," the " Pinta," driven by the storm far to the north, and finding its way with infinite difficulty into the Bay of Biscay, took refuge in the port of Bayonne. Pinzon seems to have deemed it safe to presume that the " Nina " and all its crew had been lost. Accordingly, he wrote to the monarchs of Spain, announcing the discoveries he had made, and asking permission to wait upon the court and give the particulars in person. As soon as the storm abated, he set out for the port of Palos, evidently anticipating a triumphant entry ; but when, on nearing the harbour, he beheld the ship of the Admiral, and heard the joyful acclamations with which Columbus had been received, his heart must have failed him.   It is said that he feared to go ashore, lest Columbus should put him under arrest for having deserted him on the coast of Cuba, — at least he landed privately, and kept out of sight till the Admiral had taken his departure for the Spanish court.   Deeply dejected, and broken in health, he betook himself to his home, to await the answer to the letter he had written to the king and queen.   At length the answer came.   It was reproachful in tone, and even forbade the appearance of Pinzon at court. This seemed to complete the humiliation of the old sailor, for he sank rapidly into a species of despair, and a few days later died, the victim of chagrin.

Nevertheless the services that Pinzon rendered to the expedition ought not to go unrecognized. As we have already seen, his generosity had enabled Columbus to offer to defray one eighth of the expense of the expedition. More important still, at the moment when it seemed impossible to recruit, or even conscript, a crew, it was no other than Martin Alonzo Pinzon that came forward as the earnest and successful champion of the expedition. He had been a navigator of distinction, and his wealth, his social rank, and his experience gave him an influence that withstood the tide of prejudice and made the securing of a crew possible. He not only offered to give the enterprise his moral and pecuniary support, but he gave proof of the integrity of his declarations by offering to command one of the vessels in person, while his brother was to command another. It cannot be denied that these were great and important services, without which it would have been far more difficult, if not, indeed, impossible, to put the expedition into sailing condition. But the extent of these services seems to have poisoned his mind in regard to his relations to his chief. During the voyage there were symptoms of an insubordinate spirit. The commission under which the fleet sailed gave to Columbus unquestionable authority; but Pinzon chafed under his restraints, and no sooner had they reached the coast of Cuba than he deserted his commander and undertook a voyage of discovery of his own. The sequel unfortunately showed that in spirit he was not above ignoring entirely the work of Columbus, and arrogating to himself the credit of the discovery.

Columbus, on the other hand, received in answer to his letter of announcement a most gracious reply from the Spanish sovereigns. That he was held in high favour, was shown by the simple form of the letter, which addressed him as " Don Christopher Columbus, our Admiral of the Ocean Sea, and Viceroy and Governor of the Islands discovered in the Indies." The letter expressed the great satisfaction of the monarchs with his achievement, and requested him not only to repair immediately to court, but also to inform them by return of courier what was to be done on their part to prepare the way immediately for a second expedition. Columbus lost no time in complying with their commands. He sent a memorandum of the ships, munitions, and men needed, and taking the six Indians and various curiosities he had brought with him, set out for an audience at Barcelona.

The fame of the discovery had been noised abroad, and even grossly exaggerated reports of the wonderful curiosities brought back had obtained currency. The people, therefore, everywhere thronged into the streets to get sight of Columbus and of his Indians, as they made the long journey from Palos to the court.

On reaching Barcelona the Admiral found that every preparation had been made to receive him with the most imposing ceremonials. It has been customary to compare his entrance into the city with a Roman

triumph. Certainly there was not a little to justify
such a comparison. The Indians, painted and deco-
rated in savage fashion, birds and animals of unknown
species, rare plants supposed to possess great healing
qualities, Indian coronets, bracelets, and other deco-
rations of gold, — all these were paraded and displayed in order to convey an idea of the importance
and the wealth of the newly discovered country. At
the rear of the train, Columbus, on horseback, was
escorted by a brilliant cavalcade of Spanish hidalgos.

The sovereigns had determined to receive him with
a stately ceremony worthy of his discovery. Upon a
throne specially set up for the purpose the king and
queen, with Prince Juan at their side, and surrounded
with noble lords and ladies, awaited his coming into
their presence. Columbus, also surrounded with a
brilliant retinue, entered the hall and approached the
throne. Las Casas, who was present, tells us that the
Admiral was stately and commanding in person, and
that the modest smile that played upon his countenance showed that "he enjoyed the state and glory
in which he came." Though he was probably only
forty-eight years of age, his prematurely gray hairs
had already given him a venerable appearance. The
sovereigns had made it evident that they desired to
bestow upon him the admiration and gratitude of the
nation. As he approached, they arose and saluted
him as if receiving a person of the highest rank.
When he was about to kneel, for the purpose of kiss-
ing the hands of the sovereigns, in accordance with the
conventional ceremonies of that proud court, they

ordered him in the most gracious manner to arise, and then to seat himself in their presence.

At their bidding, Columbus then proceeded to give an account of his voyage and of his discoveries. The authorities agree that this was done in a sedate and discreet manner, though it is difficult to avoid the conviction that the Admiral promised for the future far more than was warranted by anything that had as yet been discovered. But the thought was never absent from his mind that the islands were just off the coast of Asia, and that they were not far from all the wealth of Cipango and Cathay. With this belief he did not hesitate to assure their Majesties that what he had already discovered was but a harbinger of incalculable wealth, and that by further explorations whole nations and peoples would be brought to the true faith.

The contemporaneous historians tell us that at the conclusion of this account the sovereigns were so affected that their eyes filled with tears of gratitude, and that they fell upon their knees and poured forth their thanks to God for the great blessing of this discovery. The *Te Deum* was sung by the choir of the chapel, and Las Casas remarks that it seemed as if "in that hour they communicated with celestial delights."

It is not strange that in this mood the monarchs were ready, not only to continue, but even to extend the authority already bestowed upon Columbus. Accordingly, they confirmed the grants made at Santa Fé the year before, they granted him the royal

arms of Castile and Leon, and for his sake they conferred special honours on his brothers Bartholomew
and Diego. Columbus in turn committed himself to
great things in the future. His ordinary religious
fervour seems to have been greatly reinforced by the
ceremonies of the day. In his desire to promote the
conquest of the Holy Sepulchre he now went so far as
to make a solemn vow that for this purpose he would
furnish within seven years an army consisting of four
thousand horse and fifty thousand foot, and that he
would also provide a similar force within the next five
years that should follow.

It was unquestionably a weakness of Columbus that
he was always prone to promise more than he could
fulfil. This is perhaps the besetting fault of very
fervid natures. But the consequences are often far
reaching. Columbus thus prepared the way, or at
least gave the opportunity, for virulent criticism and
even hostility. Not a few of the old nobility had been
piqued by the honours conferred upon a parvenu and
a foreigner. All such were ready to organize an
attack if the new favourite should show any weakness
or fail to fulfil any of his promises. This important
element in the situation should prepare us to understand much of what is to follow.

In all affairs of international interest in the fifteenth
century the Roman pontiff played a conspicuous part.
There were unusual reasons why a formal announcement to the Pope of the success of Columbus should
be made without delay. Such announcement was
prompted, not only by the importance of the discov-

ery, but also by the religious motive that formed so
large an element in the purpose of the discoverer.
But there was an additional reason.   As we have
already seen, the king of Portugal had hinted that
the newly discovered lands, in view of the treaty of
1479, would be found to belong to himself rather
than to the monarchs of Castile and Aragon.   The
Pope was the international mediator in all questions
of this **kind.**   The Spanish sovereigns accordingly
determined to turn to the Pope without delay.

The pontiff at that time was Alexander **VI., who,**
though he has been stigmatized as having been guilty
of nearly every vice, was not unmindful of the political
significance of his position.   **Born** a subject of Aragon, he might be supposed to think favourably of the
claims of Spain ; but Ferdinand judged his character
accurately, and therefore thought it not wise to trust
anything to chance **or** accident.   Accordingly, he
despatched ambassadors **to** the court of Rome **to**
announce the new discovery with due formality, and
to set forth the gain that must **accrue** to the Church
from the acquisition of so vast a new territory.   The
ambassadors were charged to say that great care had
been taken not **to** trench upon the possessions that
had been ceded to Portugal.   On one further point
the instructions of Ferdinand were characteristic of
his great political acumen.   He desired to intimate
as delicately as possible, but at the same time with
unequivocal distinctness, that whatever the papal
pleasure might be, he should maintain and defend his
newly acquired possessions at all hazards.   This he

did by instructing his ambassadors to **say that in** the
opinion of many learned men it was not necessary
that he should obtain the papal sanction for the title
of the newly discovered lands, but that notwithstanding
this fact, as pious and devoted princes, the king and
queen supplicated his Holiness to issue **a** papal **bull**
conceding the lands which Columbus had discovered,
or hereafter might discover, to the Crown of Castile.

The news was received by Alexander with great
joy; and the request was the more readily granted
because of the favour which the Spanish sovereigns had
recently acquired at Rome by the successful termina-
tion of the terrible conflict with the Moors. Indeed,
these new discoveries appear to have been regarded
as in some sense an appropriate reward for the vigorous prosecution of that crusade against the infidels.
A bull was accordingly issued on the 2d of May, 1493,
conceding to the Spanish sovereigns the same rights
and privileges in respect to **the newly** discovered
lands in the West as had previously been granted to
the king of Portugal **in** regard to their discoveries in
Africa. In order to prevent the liability of dispute as
to jurisdiction, this bull was accompanied with another
to determine a line of demarcation. The pope **es-**
tablished **an** imaginary line "one hundred leagues
west of the Azores and Cape de Verde Islands," **ex-**
tending from **pole to pole.** All lands west of this
line that had **not** been discovered by some other
Christian power before the preceding Christmas,
and that had been or might hereafter be discovered **by** Spanish navigators, should belong **to** the

Crown of Spain; all east of that line, to the Crown of Portugal.

While these negotiations were going on with the Pope, great activity was displayed in preparation for the next voyage. In order to further the interests of Spain in the West, what in these days we should perhaps call a bureau of discovery was now established. This was placed under the superintendence of Fonseca, archdeacon of Seville, who afterward received several high ecclesiastical honours, including the patriarchate of the Indies. He was already a man of position and influence; but the writers of the time agree that he was possessed of a worldly spirit, and was devoted to temporal rather than to spiritual affairs. He seemed, however, to be so well adapted to the forming and the fitting out of armadas that, notwithstanding his high ecclesiastical dignities, the monarchs saw fit to keep him in virtual control of Indian affairs for about thirty years. Though he had great business abilities, he was capable of intense animosity, and was by no means above gratifying his private resentments in the most malignant and vindictive spirit. To assist Fonseca, Francisco Pinelo was appointed treasurer, and Juan de Soria comptroller. Their office was fixed at Seville, but the jurisdiction of the company, as we shall see, extended over a wide territory. Cadiz was made the special port of entry, with a custom-house for the new branch of maritime service.

The despotic rigour with which affairs were then kept in the hands of the government is well illustrated by the character of the orders that were issued. No one was permitted to go to the New World, either to trade or to form an establishment for other reasons, without an express license from the sovereigns, from Fonseca, or from Columbus. A still more despotic spirit was shown in the royal order commanding that "all ships in the ports of Andalusia, with their captains, pilots, and crews," should hold themselves in readiness to serve in the new expedition. Columbus and Fonseca were authorized to purchase, at their own price, any vessel that was needed, and, in case of necessity, to take it by force. They were also authorized to seize the requisite arms, provisions, and ammunitions "at any place or in any vessel in which they might be found," paying therefor such a price as they themselves might fix upon as fair and just. They were also authorized to compel, not mariners alone, but officers holding any rank or station whatsoever, to embark on their fleet, under such conditions and pay as they might deem reasonable. Finally, all civil authorities were called upon to render every assistance in expediting the armament, and were warned not to allow any impediment to be thrown in the way, on penalty of loss of office and confiscation of estate. To provide the necessary expenses, the Crown pledged two thirds of the church tithes and the sequestered property of the Jews, who, by the edict of the preceding year, had been deprived of their jewels and other possessions and ordered out of the realm. If, notwithstanding these somewhat ample resources, there should still be a lack of funds, the treasurer was authorized to con-

tract a loan. These orders were issued while Columbus was still at Barcelona, and presumably with his
approval.

Under these rigorous instructions, and in view of
the popular interest in the enterprise, preparations
for the new voyage went forward without delay. Fonseca gave himself to the collecting of vessels and their
equipment with great energy. But notwithstanding
the great resources placed at his disposal, the preparation of the fleet necessarily made slow progress.
Confronting these great powers, there were the perpetual obstacles of human nature and individual interest. Even despotism has its limitations. So much
opposition was found to be in the way of the practical confiscation of ships and munitions that it was
not until the summer was far gone that the fleet was
ready to sail. Columbus had left Barcelona on the
28th day of May; it was not till the 25th of September that the fleet were ready to weigh anchor and turn
their prows to the west.

There were special reasons why the Spanish sovereigns desired Columbus to hasten his departure on
the second voyage. A diplomatic controversy of
more than usual subtilty had sprung up between Ferdinand and Isabella and King John of Portugal.
The Portuguese monarch, probably moved by chagrin
as well as by envy, entertained a firm determination
not to abandon his claims to the new discoveries,
except from the most absolute necessity. One of the
historians of King John's reign admits that this monarch distributed bribes freely among the courtiers of

Ferdinand, and that by this means he had no difficulty in learning of the secret purposes of the Spanish court. Ambassadors were freely interchanged for the purpose of settling the questions of jurisdiction that had been raised. At one time the envoy of Ferdinand was intrusted with two communications, one of which was friendly, while the other was stern and imperative in its nature. In case he should find a pacific disposition on the part of the Portuguese king, he was to deliver the former; but if he should learn of any hostile intent to seize upon or disturb the newly discovered lands, he was to present the communication couched in peremptory terms, forbidding him to undertake any enterprise of the kind.

The import of both these communications was made known to John by his spies at the Spanish court. Accordingly, he conducted himself in such a way as to draw forth only the more pacific despatch. But notwithstanding this show of courtesy, Ferdinand had little difficulty in learning that the Portuguese monarch was planning to seize upon the new possessions before the second expedition of Columbus could reach its destination. His policy, therefore, was not only to hasten the preparations of the new expedition, but also to delay as much as possible by dilatory negotiations the movements of King John. In this latter purpose his great diplomatic acumen had full scope, and was entirely successful. He proposed that the question of their respective rights should be submitted for arbitration. The envoys consumed much time in passing with great ceremony between the two courts. King John considered it prudent neither to accept nor to decline this proposition until he had taken the precaution to make due inquiries of the Pope. The answer was what, in view of the papal bull above referred to, might have been expected. The Portuguese ambassador was informed that his Holiness would adhere to his decision establishing the line of demarcation at a hundred leagues west of the Azores. Thus Ferdinand secured a twofold triumph. The Pope had confirmed his title, and time enough had elapsed to enable the Spanish fleet to reach the disputed ground before the fleet of King John could be put in readiness to sail.

It remains to be added on this subject that King John, finding himself defeated in his attempts to gain possession of the newly discovered territories, now addressed himself to the task of having the line of demarcation extended farther to the west. In this he was more successful. After prolonged negotiations, it was finally agreed, and the agreement was embodied in the treaty of Tordesillas, June 7, 1494, that the papal line of partition should be moved to three hundred and seventy leagues west of the Cape de Verde Islands. This treaty remained in force during the age of discovery, and its importance is attested by the fact that it prevented all further discussions.

CHAPTER IV.

THE SECOND VOYAGE.

On the morning of the 25th of September, 1493, all was in readiness for the second voyage. The fleet, consisting of seventeen vessels, large and small, was at anchor in the bay of Cadiz. The scene presented a sharp contrast to that of the modest embarkation at Palos the year before. Now there was no difficulty in recruiting men; on the contrary, those who were permitted to accompany the expedition were regarded as peculiarly fortunate. Stories of the untold wealth of the new regions had been freely circulated and were very generally believed. It was the wellnigh fatal misfortune of the expedition that the men who embarked on this second voyage believed they were bound for golden regions, where nothing but wealth and the indolent pleasures of the tropics awaited them. This current but unfortunate belief determined, in large measure, the personal character of the passengers and the crew. Many of them were adventurers pure and simple; some were high-spirited hidalgos seeking romantic experiences; some were hardy mariners looking for new laurels in unknown seas;

some were visionary explorers going out simply for novelty and excitement; some were scheming speculators eager for profit at the expense of innocent natives; some were priests more or less devoutly solicitous for the conversion of the Indians and the propagation of the Catholic faith. Unfortunately, among them all there was nothing of that sturdy yeomanry which has ever been found so useful in making colonization successful.

Before sunrise the whole fleet was in motion. Steering to the southwest, in order to avoid the domains of Portugal, they arrived at the Grand Canary on the 1st of October. Here they were detained a few days in order to take in a quantity of swine, calves, goats, and sheep, with which to stock the newly discovered lands. The Admiral took the precaution of giving to each of the captains sealed orders, indicating the route to be taken, — which, however, were not to be opened except in case a vessel should lose sight of the fleet. Happily this precaution proved not to have been necessary. Weighing anchor again, the fleet, on the 7th of October, took a southwesterly course, with the purpose of making the Caribbees. After a prosperous voyage, they came upon land on the morning of the 3d of November.

The group of islands among which Columbus now found himself was the beautiful cluster which, from the eastern end of Porto Rico, bends around in the shape of a crescent toward the south, and forms a broken barrier between the main ocean and the

Caribbean Sea. The first island they reached he called Dominica, in recognition of the fact that it was discovered on Sunday; but the group as a whole, at a later period, he somewhat humorously denominated St. Ursula and the Eleven Thousand Virgins.

After cruising around several of the smaller islands, the Admiral discovered a place for safe anchorage, and went ashore. As the natives fled in confusion, the Spaniards had excellent opportunities of inspecting their ways of living. A village was found, consisting of twenty or thirty houses arranged about a hollow square. Each had its portico for shelter from the sun. Within were found hammocks of netting, utensils of earthenware, and a rude form of cotton cloth. In one of the houses was discovered a cooking utensil, apparently of iron, but probably of some kind of stone which, when burned, has a metallic lustre. But what struck the Spaniards with special interest, and even with horror, was the sight of human bones, — giving evidence, as the discoverers supposed, that they were indeed in the land of cannibals.

On the following day the boats again made a landing, — this time on an island which was named Guadaloupe, — and succeeded in capturing a boy and several women. From these Columbus learned that the inhabitants of the island were in league with the peoples of two other islands, and that this rude confederacy made war on all the rest. Its habit was to go on predatory excursions to neighbouring islands, to make prisoners of the youngest and handsomest of the women as servants and companions, and to capture men and children to be killed and eaten. It was also learned that nearly all the warriors of the island were absent. At the time of the arrival, the king, with three hundred men, was on a cruise in quest of prisoners; the women meantime, being expert archers, were left to defend their homes from invasion.

The fleet was detained for several days by the temporary loss of one of the captains and eight of his men. The commander of one of the caravels had gone on an exploring expedition, and penetrated into the forest with a part of his crew. The night passed without their return, and the greatest apprehensions were felt for their safety. Several parties were sent out in various directions in quest of them; but no tidings could be obtained. It was not until several days had elapsed, and the fleet was about to sail, that, to the joy of all, they made a signal from the shore. Their abject appearance immediately revealed how terribly they had suffered. For days they had wandered about in a vast and trackless forest, climbing mountains, fording streams, utterly bewildered, and almost in despair lest the Admiral, thinking them dead, should set sail and leave them to perish. Notwithstanding the universal joy over their return, the Admiral, with very questionable judgment, put the captain under arrest, and stopped a part of the rations of the other men. As they had strayed away without permission, Columbus thought so gross a breach of discipline should not go unpunished. It seems not to have occurred to him that the penalty had already been inflicted, and that he now had an opportunity to secure the loyalty instead of the enmity of the offenders.

On the 10th of November the Admiral hoisted anchor, and with all on board turned the ships to the northwest for La Navidad. After a few days at one of the intermediate islands, he sent a boat on shore for water and for information. The boat's crew found a village occupied exclusively by women and children. A few of these were seized and taken on board the ships. In one of the affrays, however, it was learned that the Carib women could ply their bows and arrows with amazing vigour and skill. Though the Spaniards generally covered themselves successfully with their bucklers, two of them were severely wounded. On their return to the ships, a canoe containing Carib women was upset, when, to the amazement of the Spaniards, it was found that the natives could discharge their arrows while swimming, as skilfully as though they had been upon land. One of the arrows thus discharged penetrated quite through a Spanish buckler.

It is difficult to read the original accounts of this expedition without receiving from it a very painful impression. Wherever the Spaniards landed, they must have left a remembrance of bitter enmity. Their inquiries everywhere were for gold, and their exploits were little less or more than the capture of women and children. The natives may have been cannibals indeed; but aside from all question of moral obligation, one cannot overlook the fact that they were capable of animosities, and that in consequence they were in position to help or to hinder the success of the Spanish expedition. It is not easy to understand how, as a matter of policy alone, any course could have been more unwise than that which was pursued.

It was the 22d of November before the fleet arrived off the eastern extremity of Hispaniola. Great excitement prevailed among the crew in anticipation of meeting the colonists at La Navidad. Arriving at the Gulf of Las Flechas, or, as it is now called, Semana Bay, Columbus thought it wise to send ashore one of the Indians whom the year before he had captured at this place and taken with him to Spain. The Indian had been converted to Christianity, and had learned so much of the Spanish language that the Admiral had confident hopes of his rendering important service. The native was gorgeously dressed, and loaded with trinkets with which to make a favourable impression on his countrymen. It is a significant fact that, although he made fair promises of every kind, he was never seen or heard of again. The loss was all the more important as now there was remaining with the fleet only one of the Indians that had been taken to Spain, and there was no certainty that even this one would not escape at the first opportunity.

On the 25th the Admiral cast anchor in the harbour of Monte Christi, desirous of taking further observations about the mouth of the stream which, in the former voyage, he had called the Rio del Oro, or the

Golden River. But all the pleasant anticipations of the adventurers now began to be overcast with gloomy forebodings. On the banks they discovered two dead bodies, with arms extended and bound by the wrists to a wooden stake in the form of a cross. Other evidences were not wanting to warrant the fear that some misfortune had befallen Arana and his companions. Two days later, anchors were dropped off the harbour of Navidad. Cannon were fired; but there came back no welcoming response. There was no sign of life, — nothing but a deathlike silence. It was now evident that disaster had overtaken the colony. On the following day the terrible fact was revealed that every member had perished.

The first shock occasioned by this information was, however, slightly alleviated by the friendly bearing of the natives. At first it was feared that there had been treachery on the part of the Indians in whom the Admiral had reposed confidence and friendship; but the accounts given by the natives tended to dispel this fear, and to convince the Spaniards that the colonists had perished from other causes. Some of them, it was said, had died of sickness; some had fallen in quarrels among themselves; and some, having gone to other parts of the island, had taken Indian wives and adopted the customs of the natives. These accounts justified the hope that some of the garrison were yet alive, and might return to the fleet and give an account, not only of the disaster, but also of the interior of the island.

But on going ashore to reconnoitre, Columbus

found very little reason for comfort or hope. The fortress was a ruin, the palisades were beaten down, the chests were broken open, the provisions were spoiled, — in short, the whole settlement presented the appearance of having been sacked and destroyed. Here and there were to be found broken utensils and torn garments, but no traces of the garrison were to be seen. Cannon were fired, but no response was awakened, and nothing but a mournful silence reigned over the desolation.

Columbus had ordered Arana, in case of attack or danger, to secrete the treasure in a well; but all their efforts to discover where anything had been concealed were now in vain. It was not until the search had been kept up for several days that even dead bodies were found. Suspicions were revived that there had been treachery on the part of the cacique; but a little exploration resulted in the discovery that the tribal village of that official had also shared in the disaster that had befallen the garrison.

Little by little the general facts of the calamity came to be known. The colony, with the exception of the commander, was made up of men of the lowest order. The list included a considerable number of mariners that were given to every kind of excess and turbulence. Surrounded by savage tribes, they were dependent on the good-will of the natives, as well as on their own prudence and good conduct. Oviedo assures us that they soon fell into every species of wanton abuse. Some were prompted by unrestrained avarice, and some by gross sensuality.

Not content with the two or three wives apiece which the good-natured cacique allowed them, they gave themselves up to the most unbridled license with the wives and daughters of the Indians. The natural consequences followed. Fierce brawls ensued over their ill-gotten spoils and the favours of the Indian women. The injunctions of Columbus that they should keep together in the fortress and maintain military order were neglected and forgotten. Many deserted the garrison, and lived at random among the natives. These were gradually formed into groups, to protect themselves and despoil the rest. Violent affrays ensued. One company, under the command of a subordinate officer, set out for the mines of Cibao, of which, from the first, they had heard marvellous accounts. The region to which they went was in the eastern part of the island, — a territory governed by Caonabo, a Carib chieftain famous for his fierce and warlike exploits. He was the hero of the island ; and the departure of Columbus gave him an opportunity to rid the country of those who threatened to eclipse his authority. When now his territory was actually invaded, he determined to exterminate the colony. The campaign appears not to have been a long or difficult one. The cacique of the region surrounding La Navidad was faithful to his promises, and fought with the Spaniards against the Carib chieftain. But even their united efforts were unsuccessful. The local cacique, Guacanagari, and his subjects fought faithfully in defence of their guests, but they were soon overpowered. Some of

the Spaniards were killed in the struggle, some were
driven into the sea and drowned, some were mas-
sacred on shore; not a single one was ever heard
of again alive.

The cacique Guacanagari continued to manifest
his friendly interest in Columbus and his crew,
though it was evident that his belief in the heavenly
origin and character of the Spaniards had been sadly
shaken. It is said that the gross licentiousness of the
garrison had already impaired his veneration for the
heaven-born visitors. When, therefore, Columbus proposed to establish a permanent settlement in the region,
Guacanagari expressed his satisfaction, but observed
that the region was unhealthy, and that perhaps the
Spaniards could do better in some other locality.

While these parleyings were going on, an event
occurred of interesting and even romantic significance. The cacique visited the ship of the Admiral,
and was greatly interested in all that he saw. Among
other objects of curiosity were the women whom the
visitors had taken as prisoners on the Caribbean
Islands. One of these, who by reason of her stately
beauty had been named Catilina, particularly attracted the interest and admiration of the chieftain.
Several days later, a brother of the cacique came on
board under pretence of bargaining gold for Spanish
trinkets. In the course of his visit he succeeded in
having an interview with Catilina. At midnight, just
before the fleet was about to sail, the tropical beauty
awakened her companions. Though the ship was
anchored three miles from land and the sea was

rough, they let themselves down by the sides of the vessel, and swam vigorously for the shore. The watchmen, however, were awakened, and a boat was quickly sent out in pursuit. But the skill and vigour of the women were such that they reached the land in safety. Though four of them were retaken on the beach, Catilina and the rest of her companions made good their escape to the forest. On the following day, when Columbus sent to demand of Guacanagari the return of the fugitives, it was found that the cacique had removed his effects and his followers to the interior. This sudden departure confirmed the suspicion in the mind of Columbus that Guacanagari was a traitor to the Spaniards ; he even thought that the chief had been the perfidious betrayer of the garrison.

This suspicion made Columbus all the more willing to seek another spot for a permanent settlement. After some days spent in explorations, it was determined to establish a post at about ten leagues east of La Navidad, where they found a spacious harbour, protected on one side by a natural rampart of rocks, and on the other by an impervious forest, as Bernaldez says, " so close that a rabbit could hardly make his way through it." A green and beautiful plain, extending back from the sea, was watered by two rivers, which promised to furnish the needed power for mills. The streams abounded in fish, the soil was covered with an exuberant vegetation, and the climate appeared to be temperate and genial. This site had the further advantage of proximity to the gold mines in the mountains of Cibao.

Here the first American city was projected, to which Columbus, in honour of the queen, gave the name of Isabella. Streets and squares were promptly laid out; a church, a public storehouse, and a residence for the Admiral were begun without delay. The public houses were built of stone, while those intended for private occupation were constructed of wood, plaster, and such other materials as the situation afforded.

It was not long, however, before there was abundant evidence that the colony was made up of men very ill adapted to the peculiar hardships of the situation. The labour of clearing lands, building houses, and planting orchards and gardens can be successfully carried on only by men accustomed to vigorous manual labour. The stagnant and malarious atmosphere bore hard upon those who had been accustomed to old and highly cultivated lands. Long after landing, moreover, the Spaniards were obliged to subsist very largely upon salt food and mouldy bread. It is not strange that the maladies peculiar to new countries broke out with violence. Disaffections of mind also became wellnigh universal. Many of the adventurers had embarked with the expectation of finding the golden regions of Cipango and Cathay, where fortunes were to be accumulated without effort. Instead of the realization of these hopes, they now found that they were doomed to struggle with the hard conditions of Nature, and to toil painfully

for the merest subsistence. What with the ravages
of disease and the general gloom of despondency,
the situation soon became painful indeed. Even the
strength of Columbus himself was obliged finally to
succumb to the cares and anxieties of the situation.
But though for several weeks he was confined to his
bed by illness, he still had the fortitude to give directions about the building of the city and the superin-
tending of the general affairs of the colony.

The situation was indeed depressing. Columbus
had hoped that soon after reaching his destination he
should be able to send back to Spain glowing reports
of what had been accomplished by the settlers at
La Navidad, as well as in regard to his own discoveries. But the destruction of the colony had now
rendered such a report impossible. In order, however, to relieve the disappointment at home as much
as possible, he determined to send out two exploring
expeditions, in the hope that the cities and mines, of
which he had heard and dreamed so much, might be
discovered. He was still ardent in the belief that
the island of Hispaniola was none other than Cipango, and that somewhere not far away would be
found the cities of boundless wealth of which Marco
Polo and Toscanelli had written.

To lead the two expeditions of discovery, Columbus
selected two cavaliers by the name of Ojeda and
Gorvalan. The former had already, before leaving
Spain, made himself famous for his daring spirit and
great vigour and agility of body. The latter seems
also to have been well adapted to the task before

him. The expeditions pressed southward into the very heart of the island. That of Ojeda was the more interesting and the more important. After climbing the adjacent mountain range, the explorers found themselves on the edge of a vast plain, or *vega*, that was studded with villages and hamlets. The inhabitants were everywhere hospitable. Five or six days were needed to cross the plain and reach the chain of mountains that were said to enclose the golden region of Cibao. Caonabo, the redoubtable chief of the region, nowhere appeared to dispute their passage. The natives everywhere received the explorers with kindness, and pointed out to them numerous evidences of natural wealth. Particles of shining gold were seen in the mountain-streams, and if we may believe the chroniclers of the time, Ojeda himself, in one of the brooks, picked up a large mass of native metal. As the object of the expedition was merely to explore the nature of the country, Ojeda was now satisfied with the result, and accordingly he led back his band of explorers to the fleet. He gave a glowing account of the golden resources of the island, and his story was corroborated by the report of Gorvalan. Columbus decided at once to send back a report to the Spanish monarchs. Twelve of the ships were ordered to put themselves in readiness for the return voyage.

The report sent by Columbus was one of great importance. He described the exploring expeditions in glowing terms, and repeated his former hopes of being able soon to make abundant shipments of

gold and other articles of value. Special stress was
laid on the beauty and fertility of the land, including its adaptation to the raising of the various
grains and vegetables produced in Europe. Time,
however, would be required, he said, to obtain the
provisions necessary for subsistence from the fields
and gardens; and therefore the colonists must rely,
for a considerable time to come, upon shipments from
home. He then enumerated the articles that would
be especially needed. He censured the contractors
that had furnished the wine, charging them with using
leaky casks, and then called for an additional number
of workmen and mechanics and men skilled in the
working of ores.

This interesting report is still preserved, with the
comments of the Spanish sovereigns written on the
margins. To the descriptions of what had been
done, as well as to the recommendations for the future, commendation and assent were given in generous
and complimentary terms. One or two passages are
of exceptional interest. In regard to the wine,
Columbus writes, —

" A large portion of the wine that we brought with us
has run away, in consequence, as most of the men say, of
the bad cooperage of the butts made at Seville; the article that we stand most in need of now, and shall stand in
need of, is wine."

To this declaration, which would seem to be good
evidence that dishonest or negligent contractors are
not the peculiarity of the nineteenth century, the
following was the royal response : —

" Their Highnesses will give instructions to Don Juan de Fonseca to make inquiry respecting the imposition in the matter of the casks, in order that those who supplied them shall, at their own expense, make good the loss occasioned by the waste of the wine, together with the costs."

But the most interesting, as well as the most significant part of the report is that which pertains to what was nothing less than a purpose to open a slave-trade on a large scale between the islands and the mother-country. In a former portion of the letter, Columbus had already called attention to the advantages that would flow from a system of sending slaves to Spain to be educated in the Spanish language, and then brought back to the islands as interpreters. To this proposal the royal assent was given in the following characteristic words : —

" He has done well, and let him do what he says ; but let him endeavour by all possible means to connect them to our holy Catholic religion, and do the same with respect to the inhabitants of all the islands to which he may go."

But to the more elaborate and systematic proposal, a different answer was returned. The paragraph of the memorial containing the proposition is so curious a combination of sophistry and good motives that it will bear quoting as a whole. The reader should perhaps be reminded that although the paper was intended for the king and queen, it was addressed to Antonio de Torres, as ambassador. The following is the language of Columbus : —

"You will tell their Highnesses that the welfare of the souls of the said cannibals, and the inhabitants of this island also, has suggested the thought that the greater number that are sent over to Spain the better, and thus good service may result to their Highnesses in the following manner. Considering what great need we have of cattle and beasts of burden, both for food and to assist the settlers in this and all these islands, both for peopling the land and cultivating the soil, their Highnesses might authorize a suitable number of caravels to come here every year to bring over said cattle and provisions and other articles; these cattle, etc., might be sold at moderate prices for account of the bearers, and the latter might be paid with slaves taken from among the Caribbees, who are a wild people, fit for any work, well proportioned and very intelligent, and who, when they have got rid of the cruel habits to which they have been accustomed, will be better than any other kind of slaves. When they are out of their country, they will forget their cruel customs; and it will be easy to obtain plenty of these savages by means of row-boats that we propose to build. It is taken for granted that each of the caravels sent by their Highnesses will have on board a confidential man, who will take care that the vessels do not stop anywhere else than here, where they are to unload and reload their vessels. Their Highnesses might fix duties on the slaves that may be taken over, upon their arrival in Spain. You will ask for a reply upon this point, and bring it to me, in order that I may be able to take the necessary measures, should the proposition merit the approbation of their Highnesses."

To this elaborate scheme for reducing the natives to slavery the sovereigns gave the diplomatic answer characteristic of those who would say no in a manner that would give the least offence. The royal language was the following : —

"The consideration of this subject has been suspended for a time until further advices arrive from the other side; let the Admiral write more fully what he thinks upon the matter."

The authority asked for certainly was not granted; but, on the other hand, there was no intimation that the proposition would, in the end, meet with a refusal. Columbus seems to have thought it not imprudent to take advantage of the doubt; for Bernaldez tells us that the Admiral "made incursions into the interior, and captured vast numbers of the natives; and the second time that he sent home, he sent five hundred Indian men and women, all in the flower of their age, between twelve years and thirty-five or thereabouts, all of whom were delivered at Seville to Don Juan de Fonseca." "They came," continued Bernaldez, "as they went about in their own country, naked as they were born; from which they experienced no more embarrassment than the brutes." "They were sold," the narrator adds, "but proved of very little service, for the greater part of them died of the climate."

Of interesting significance also are the passages and answers relating to gold. In one of the paragraphs Columbus calls attention to the fact that although the gold discovered has been found in the streams, it must have come from the earth, and that the procuring of it will involve the delay necessarily

attending the establishment of mining operations.
He recommends that labourers in considerable numbers be sent out from the quicksilver mines. To
these suggestions the king responds, —

"It is the most necessary thing possible that he should
strive to find the way to this gold."

And to the suggestion in regard to the mines he
responds, —

"This shall be completely provided for in the next
voyage out; meanwhile Don Juan de Fonseca has their
Highnesses' orders to send as many miners as he can
find. Their Highnesses write also to Almaden with
instructions to select the greatest number that can be
procured, and to send them up."

After the departure of the vessels for Spain, the
Admiral, having for the most part recovered his
health, determined to make an expedition in person
into the heart of the island. Accordingly, on the
12th of March, 1494, he set out with the requisite
number of men, foot and horse, for the province of
Cibao. This region was distant about eighteen
leagues. To reach his destination it was necessary
to cross the beautiful plain which had already been
described by Ojeda, and to which the Admiral now
gave the name of Royal Vega. On the border of
Cibao he decided to build a fortress, which should be
at once a protection and a rallying-point. The natives as yet continued to be friendly, and came in
considerable numbers to barter bits of gold for such
trinkets as the Spaniards might give in exchange.

The gold mines, however, seemed to be as far away as ever, although glowing accounts were given by the natives of the nuggets that were to be discovered beyond the mountains.   But instead of completing his explorations in person, Columbus now determined to return to the fleet and make a voyage to what he supposed to be the continent.   The fortress, to which he gave the name St. Thomas, was intrusted to a garrison under the command of Margarite, an officer of high rank and much experience.

It is of interest to note at this point that the early opinions of the Spaniards in regard to the Indians had slowly undergone a very considerable change. Further acquaintance had convinced Columbus that they were not quite so guileless and docile as at first he had supposed them to be.   They were found to know something of war, — at least to be acquainted with certain rude methods of attack and defence. The proximity of the Caribs was giving them a constant schooling in the art of self-protection.

It is at this point that Bernaldez, a companion and friend of Columbus, gives an interesting account of the products of the islands and of some of the peculiarities of the natives.   The following passage is perhaps the most graphic and circumstantial account left us by any contemporaneous writer : —

"As the people of all these islands are destitute of iron, it is wonderful to see their tools, which are of stone, very sharp and admirably made, such as axes, adzes, and other instruments, which they use in constructing their dwellings.   Their food is bread, made from roots, which

God has given them instead of wheat; for they have neither wheat nor rye, nor barley, nor oats, nor spelt-wheat, nor panic-grass, nor anything resembling them. No kind of food that the Castilians had as yet tasted was like anything that we have here. There were no beans, nor chick-peas, nor vetches, nor lentils, nor lupines, nor any quadruped or animal, excepting some small dogs, and the others, which look like large rats, or something between a large rat and a rabbit, and are very good and savoury for eating, and have feet and paws like rats, and climb trees. The dogs are of all colours, — white, black, etc. There are lizards and snakes, but not many, for the Indians eat them, and think them as great a dainty as partridges are to the Castilians. The lizards are like ours in size, but different in shape, though, in a little island near the harbour called San Juan, where the squadron remained several days, a lizard was several times seen, as large round as a young calf, and as smooth as a lance; and several times they attempted to kill it, but could not, on account of the thickness of the trees, and it fled into the sea. Besides eating lizards and snakes, these Indians devour all the spiders and worms that they find, so that their beastliness appears to exceed that of any beast."

Modern investigation has thrown much light on the physical characteristics of the native inhabitants of the Lucayan or Bahama islands. Some years ago Ecker and Wyman studied the subject, and more recently Prof. W. K. Brooks has visited the islands and presented a memoir to the National Academy of Sciences on the peculiarities of the bones discovered in the course of his investigations. It is clearly established that the natives belonged to a large and well-developed race.   Ecker found bones which he thought must have belonged to a race of giants.   But Professor Brooks is of the opinion that they "did not depart essentially from the Spanish average."   His measurements showed that "The skulls are large, and about equal in size to the average modern civilized white skull."

It is pathetic to reflect that this race was, in a few years, swept completely out of existence by the methods of the Spaniards.   The annals of cruelty present no darker picture than that given us by Las Casas, who at the time was a sad witness of what was taking place.   The five shiploads of slaves sent back by Columbus in the course of his second expedition was but the beginning of a policy which did not end till the six hundred islands of the Bahamas were completely depopulated.   The work begun by the Admiral was completed by bloodhounds in less than a generation.   The race perished, and may be said to have left only a single word as a monument.   The Spaniards took from them the word "hammock," and gave it to all the languages of western Europe.

After Columbus returned to Isabella from St. Thomas he devoted himself for some days to putting the colony in order, preparatory to his own departure on a further voyage of discovery.   Second only to the desire of Ferdinand and Isabella for gold, was their wish that Columbus should devote himself, as far as possible, to further discoveries.   This disposition, so perfectly in accord with the enterprising

spirit of the Admiral, was fostered by a common
jealousy of the Portuguese; for while the ships of
Columbus, after going westward, were exploring what
they supposed to be the islands of the East, the
fleets of John II. of Portugal were making their way
toward India by going eastward. The more rapidly,
therefore, each nation could advance, the more of the
" much-coveted lands " each nation would hereafter
be able to claim. Acting in accordance with this
impulse and policy, Columbus was determined to leave
the garrisons at Isabella and St. Thomas, and, with
a sufficient crew, proceed to explore and plant his
standards on what he confidently supposed to be the
continent.

This purpose was in many respects unfortunate;
for the garrisons were in no condition to be intrusted
with the independent working out of their own des-
tiny. There was wellnigh universal discontent. It
is easy to imagine the condition of affairs. Sickness
everywhere prevailed. The encampments — for they
were little else — were, as we must not forget, made up
of men of all ranks and stations. Some were hidalgos,
some were men who had been attached to the court,
some were common labourers; but all men, high and
low, were obliged to labour with their hands, under
regulations that were strictly enforced. Many had
joined the expedition in the belief that they would
find gold in abundance; but now they found sickness
and hardships of the most exacting kind. These
discontents found expression at length in a mutinous
spirit that threatened to seize the ships and leave

Columbus alone to his fate. The chief mutineer, Bernald Diaz, was seized and sent for trial to Spain. But the disappointments were so numerous and so intense that many members of the expedition, especially those high in rank, thinking that Columbus had deceived them, not only charged him with all their discomforts, but even showed a relentless disposition to pursue him to his ruin. It was with this state of affairs, impending or actually in existence, that Columbus, on the 24th of April, 1494, hoisted sail for Cuba and the other lands in the west. His brother Diego was left in command at Isabella.

On approaching the easternmost point of Cuba the fleet turned to the left, with the intention of exploring the southern coast, instead of the northern, as the Admiral had done in the first voyage. Bernaldez, who probably often talked the matter over with Columbus, distinctly tells us that it was the object of the Admiral to find the province and city of Cathay. The naive and confident statement of this historian is worthy of note, for it doubtless reflected the belief entertained by Columbus till the day of his death. Bernaldez says: "This province is in the dominion of the Grand Kahn, and, as described by John de Mandeville and others who have seen it, is the richest province in the world, and the most abundant in gold and silver and other metals, and silks. The people are all idolaters, and are a very acute race, skilled in necromancy, learned in all the arts and courtesies; and of this place many marvels are written, which may be found in the narrative of the noble English knight, John de Mandeville, who visited the country, and lived for some time with the Grand Kahn." And then, after stating how it was that, in his opinion, Columbus missed his mark, he says: "And so I told him, and made him know and understand, in the year 1496, when he first returned to Castile after this expedition, and when he was my guest, and left with me some of his papers in the presence of Juan de Fonseca. . . . From these papers," he continues, "I have drawn and have compared them with others, which were written by that honourable gentleman, the Doctor Chanca, and other noble gentlemen who came with the Admiral in the voyages already described."

Bernaldez also tells us that Columbus at first supposed the land, which he called Juana, but which the natives called Cuba, to be an island, and that it was not until he had made a voyage along the coast that he inferred confidently that it was the mainland. To the questions of the Admiral on this subject, the Indians were able to give no satisfactory answer; "for," says Bernaldez, "they are a stupid race, who think that all the world is an island, and do not know what a continent is."

The westward sail was continued, with some interruptions, from the 1st of May till the 12th of June, without any occurrence sufficiently remarkable to require extended notice. One statement of exceptional interest, however, is made by the writer already so frequently quoted. Bernaldez says that "at this point it occurred to the Admiral that, if he should be

prospered, he might succeed in returning to Spain by
the East, going to the Ganges, thence to the Arabian
Gulf, by land, from Ethiopia to Jerusalem and to
Joppa, whence he might embark on the Mediterranean, and arrive at Cadiz." Although, in the opinion
of the narrator, this passage would be possible, he says
it would be very perilous ; " for from Ethiopia to Jerusalem, the inhabitants are all Moors." He rightly
inferred that so near the close of the Moorish wars,
the Spaniards would do well not to intrust themselves
to the vicissitudes of a journey through Arabia.

On the 12th of June the mutinous spirit of the
crew was so general that the Admiral decided to turn
back. It is easy to understand that he did so with
great reluctance. He had determined to reach the
continent, and if possible go to Cathay, the home
of that luxury and wealth which had so excited the
readers of John de Mandeville. Would he now return
and confess to failure? In order to answer this
question, he resorted to a device that must ever
remain as a conspicuous stigma, not only upon his
character, but also upon his good sense. He resolved
to establish a geographical fact by a certificate under
oath. He drew up the eighty men of his crew, and
required them to swear before a notary that it was
possible to go from Cuba to Spain by land. Accordingly, it was solemnly sworn that Cuba was a part of
the mainland, — that is to say, Cathay ; and it was
further ordered that if any sceptic should deny this
important fact, he should be fined ten thousand maravedis. If any lack of faith in this great geographical

fact should disclose itself on the part of any common sailor, the culprit, as he would, of course, not have the money, was to have a hundred lashes, and then be incapacitated for further lying by having his tongue pulled out.

In the course of this voyage, Columbus made many discoveries, among them the island of Jamaica and the group known as the Garden of the Queen. Among these islands the ships often ran aground, and the difficulties of navigation were such that for many days the Admiral is said to have secured no sleep whatever. At length, however, an unconquerable drowsiness and illness came on, which left him helpless in the hands of the crew. Taking advantage of this situation, the mariners turned the ships toward Isabella, where they arrived, after an absence of more than five months, on the 29th of September. The fruits of the voyage were several discoveries of important islands, and a further and wider knowledge of the characteristics of the natives. There was, however, no clew to any gold mines or other resources that might be profitably taken back to Spain.

The illness of Columbus continued during five months after his return to Isabella. It was fortunate that in the course of his voyage of exploration the colony was visited by his brother Bartholomew. But affairs were in a sad state of confusion. During the absence of the Admiral, everything had seemed to contribute to a general disorganization. This unfortunate state of the colony was partly owing to a very injudicious order issued by Columbus, and partly to the unwise methods of administration that had prevailed during his absence.

Columbus before going away had ordered the military commander, Margarite, to put himself at the head of four hundred men and go through the country for the twofold purpose of obtaining provisions and of impressing upon the natives a further respect for Spanish power. Of the instructions given there were only two provisions that seem to have been important. In the first place, they were to obtain provisions, — by purchase, if possible, if not, by any other means; and secondly, they were to capture, either by force or artifice, Caonabo and his brothers.

Fernando Columbus tells us that Margarite, instead of striving to overrun and reduce the island, took his soldiers into the great plain known as the Royal Vega, and there gave them up to all forms of wanton excesses. But he soon fell into disputes with the council instituted by the Admiral. After sending its members insolent letters, and finding that he could not reduce them to obedience, he went aboard one of the first ships that came from Spain, and sailed for home. This he appears to have done without giving any account of himself, or leaving any direction in regard to his command. "Upon this," says Fernando, "every one went away among the Indians wherever he thought fit, taking away their goods and their women, and committing such outrages that the Indians resolved to be revenged on those they found alone or straggling; so that the cacique had killed ten, and

privately ordered a house to be fired in which were
eleven sick." The same authority further states that
" Most of the Christians committed a thousand insolences, for which they were mortally hated by the
Indians, who refused to submit to them."

Such was the condition of affairs on the return of
Columbus. All was in such confusion that the very
existence of the colony was threatened with the fate
that had overtaken La Navidad ; and it was for essentially the same cause. The weakness of Margarite and his subsequent desertion of his command
had thrown the garrison into anarchy, and given it
up to the unbridled indulgence of the most provoking
and offensive excesses. Fernando Columbus himself says of the Indians that in consequence of the
" thousand insolences " of the Christians, " it was no
difficult matter for them all to agree to cast off the
Spanish yoke." That the provocation was chargeable
to the Spaniards is admitted both by Don Fernando
and by Las Casas. But the fact that the invaders
had brought this threatening condition of affairs upon
themselves can hardly be thought to have lessened
the obligations of Columbus. What he was now
confronted with was a condition, not a theory as to
how that condition had been brought about. In
order to save the colony from immediate and perhaps fatal disaster, he was obliged to act without
hesitation.

While Caonabo was threatening the garrison at
St. Thomas, another of the caciques, Gustignana by
name, approached with a large force to within two

days' march of Isabella.   It is even said that his
army consisted of a hundred thousand men.   Columbus was able to muster a hundred and sixty Spanish foot, twenty horsemen, and as many bloodhounds.
The force was divided into two battalions, one being
under the command of the Admiral himself, and the
other under that of his brother Bartholomew.   The
Spaniards were clad in armour, while the natives had
only their naked bodies to oppose to the ferocity of
the bloodhounds and the cross-bows and musketry
of the invaders.   At the first onset the Indians were
thrown into confusion, and a terrible carnage ensued.
Vast numbers were either killed outright or torn by
the dogs ; while others, perhaps less fortunate, were
taken prisoners, to be sent to Spain as slaves.   The
force of the Indians was completely broken up and
dispersed ; but Caonabo, who was besieging St.
Thomas, was still at large.

This Carib chieftain was very naturally a source of
great anxiety to the Admiral.   He had been defeated
by Ojeda ; but he was still at the head of a formidable
force, and his own intrepidity and skill made him
a constant object of dread.   Columbus determined
to secure him by treachery.   Ojeda was selected to
carry out this purpose ; and the instructions given
by the Admiral were base and treacherous in the
extreme.   The wily Spanish officer was to beguile
the Indian chieftain to a friendly interview ; and thus,
having thrown him off his guard, was to put him in
irons and escape with him to the Spanish garrison.
The Admiral's plan was carried out.

The accounts of this ignoble transaction, as given by Las Casas and the later historians of the time, do not differ in essential particulars, though there are differences in unimportant details. The authorities, moreover, are not agreed as to the time when this daring exploit occurred. Herrera says that it took place before the great battle, almost immediately after the return of Columbus from Cuba. Attributing the design to the Admiral, this historian says, " He contrived to send Alonzo de Ojeda with only nine Spaniards, under colour of carrying a present." According to the same authority, the capture took place about sixty or seventy leagues from Isabella. Herrera's account is graphic and circumstantial. Other authorities tell us that it was the last act required to reduce the island into subjection. But the precise date is not important. Las Casas, who visited the island six years after the event took place, and received his information on the spot, has preserved the account which has generally been followed by the subsequent annalists and historians.

It is not difficult to understand how the friendly relations which at first prevailed between the Spaniards and the Indians were gradually converted into distrust, and finally into deadly hostility. For this change the Spaniards must ever be held responsible. All the original accounts agree that the natives of Hispaniola were remarkable alike for their gentleness, their friendliness, and their generosity, and that they looked upon the Spaniards as superior beings that had descended from heaven. The son of the

Admiral himself tells us that as time passed on, the Spaniards were guilty of " a thousand insolences, especially to the Indian women." We have already seen how Columbus sent home five shiploads of inoffensive natives of Hispaniola to be sold in the Spanish markets.

It was easy now for the invaders to go one step farther in this process of subjugation. The capture of Caonabo had removed the last serious obstacle to a complete control of the island. Fernando tells us that the country now became so peaceable that " one single Christian went safely wherever he pleased." Supreme power was now in the hand of the Admiral, and he determined to make use of it in the interest of that great object of his expedition which as yet had been completely unsuccessful.

In order that the call for gold might at length be gratified, he determined to impose a tribute on all the population of the island. The matter was thus provided for: Every Indian above fourteen years old who was in the vicinity of the mines was required to pay every three months a little bellful of gold, and to take for it a brass or tin token, and to wear this about the neck, as a receipt or evidence that payment had been made. All persons not living in the vicinity of the mines were every three months to pay twenty-five pounds of cotton.

When this order was issued, the natives were thrown into something like despair. They asserted that they knew not how to collect the gold, and that the gathering of so large an amount would be impos-

sible. The cacique of the Royal Vega tried to persuade the Admiral to modify the order. He offered
to convert the whole of the Royal Vega, stretching
from Isabella to the sea on the opposite shore, into
a huge farm, which would supply the whole of Castile
with bread, on condition that the tribute in gold
should be relaxed; but Columbus would not accept
the proposition, as he wished to collect such objects
of value as he could take back to Spain.

It was found impossible to enforce the requirements imposed. The gold in requisite amounts could
not be found. Columbus was therefore obliged to
modify his demands. In some instances the amounts
called for were lessened; in some the nature of the
demand was modified; in others service was accepted in place of tribute.

As time passed on, it was found that personal service was the only form of tax that could readily be
enforced; and, accordingly, more and more the natives were driven into working the farms of the Spanish settlements. As early as 1496 the fields of the
Spaniards had come to be very generally tilled and
harvested in this manner. Out of this form of taxa-
tion grew the system of *repartimientos,* or *enco-
miendas,* as they were afterward called. In order
to enforce the payment of such tributes as were required, four forts in addition to those of Isabella and
St. Thomas were built and equipped, at such points
as would give most complete command and control
of the island.

It requires no very vivid imagination to enable one

to understand the desperate situation into which the natives found they had been driven. They had enjoyed a roving independence and that ample leisure which is so dear to all the aboriginal inhabitants of the tropics. This pleasant life was now at an end; the yoke of servitude was fastened upon them, and there was no prospect save in the thraldom of perpetual slavery. They were obliged to bend their bodies under the fervour of a tropical sun, either to raise food for their taskmasters, or to sift the sands of the streams for the shining grains of gold. Peter Martyr relates, with an unspeakable pathos, how their sorrows and sufferings wove themselves into doleful songs and ballads, and how with plaintive tunes and mournful voices they bewailed the servitude into which they had been thrown.

At last they determined to avail themselves of a most desperate remedy. They observed how entirely dependent the Spaniards were upon such food as was supplied by the natives. They now agreed, by a general concert of action, not to cultivate the articles of food, and to destroy those already growing, in order by famine to starve the strangers or drive them from the island. This policy was carried into effect. They abandoned their homes, laid waste the fields, and withdrew to the mountains, where they hoped to subsist on roots and herbs.

Although this policy produced some distress among the Spaniards, still they had the resources of home; and it is certain that the suffering of the natives even from hunger was far greater than was the suffering of the invaders. The Spaniards pursued the Indians from one retreat to another, following them into caverns, pursuing them into thick forests, and driving them up mountain heights, until, worn out with fatigue and hunger, the wretched creatures gave themselves up without conditions to the mercy of their pursuers. After thousands of them had perished miserably through famine, fatigue, disease, and terror, the survivors abandoned all opposition, and bent their necks despairingly to the yoke.

While this pitiful state of affairs was taking place on the island, matters of equal significance and interest were occurring in Spain ; and it is now necessary that we turn our attention thither in order to understand the meaning of that disfavour into which Columbus was now rapidly drifting.

Even after the second voyage was undertaken, there were not a few who ventured to declare that Columbus had been cruel and unjust to his subordinates, and that the assurances and promises by means of which the second fleet had been fitted out, were such as never could be fulfilled. The malcontents included persons high in royal favour ; and even Fonseca, who, as we have seen, had been made a special minister or secretary for the Indies, looked upon the Admiral with distrust, if not with positive disfavour. There was also about the royal court a nucleus of opposition consisting of members of the old nobility, who saw their own hereditary significance completely eclipsed by this untitled adventurer from abroad. Here, then, was a fertile soil ready to re-

ceive any seed of accusation or complaint that might
be brought back from the newly discovered lands.
Such accusations and complaints were not long
withheld.

The provisions taken out on the second voyage
were not abundant in amount, and many of them, as
we have already seen, were spoiled or injured in the
course of the passage. On reaching Hispaniola, and
finding that the colony at La Navidad had perished,
it became immediately evident that new supplies must
be obtained. The Admiral was naturally reluctant
to call upon the Government for further assistance.
Although such a course was found to be absolutely
necessary, the demand was made as small as possible,
in the hope that a large portion of the articles
needed could be either raised or bought on the
island. In the interests of this policy the most rigorous methods were adopted to increase the productive
force of the colony. In the building of Isabella, and
in the tilling of the fields, many a delicate hand that
had never touched an implement of industry was now
forced into manual labour. It is not necessary to in-
quire whether Columbus enforced his rule with impo-
litic or unnecessary rigour. It is certain, however,
that discontents became rife, that these soon grew to
formidable proportions and finally ripened into a
mutinous determination to throw off the Admiral's
authority. By good fortune, Columbus discovered
the mutinous intent before the final outbreak; but
the purpose was so widespread, and embraced within
its plans so many of the officers high in command,

that he felt obliged, not only to put the leaders in irons, but also to transfer all the guns, ammunition, and naval stores to his own ship. Herrera tells us that "this was the first mutiny that occurred in the Indies," and that "it was the source of all the opposition the Admiral and his successors met withal."

But the suppression of the mutiny did not lessen the discontents. One of the authorities says: "The better sort were obliged to work, which was as bad as death to them, especially having little to eat." The Admiral had recourse to force, and this deepened the ill-will. One of the priests, Father Boyle, took up the cause of the malcontents, and was loud in his accusations of cruelty. Herrera tells us that so many persons of distinction died of starvation and sickness that, long after Isabella was abandoned, "so many dreadful cries were heard in that place that people durst not go that way."

Another cause of discontent was the fact that Columbus placed so great authority in the hands of his brothers. Diego Columbus had attended the Admiral on his second voyage, and on arriving at Hispaniola, was made second in command. The other brother, Bartholomew, reached the colony while the Admiral was exploring Cuba and Jamaica. Far abler and wiser than Diego, Bartholomew was at once, on the return of the Admiral, raised to the rank of Adelantado, or Lieutenant-Governor. Bartholomew is described as "somewhat harsh in his temper, very brave and free, for which some hated him." The Spanish hidalgos always looked upon Columbus as a foreigner, and the favour he showed his brothers only tended to deepen their discontents and multiply their complaints.

Added to all other sources of dissatisfaction was the most potent fact of all, — that the amount of gold sent home as compared with what had been promised, was doubtful in quality and insignificant in amount. Indeed, the first assayer who accompanied the expedition even declared that the metal discovered was not gold, but only a base imitation.

Such were the grounds of ill-feeling in the colony, and from time to time they were reported to friends in the mother-country. We have already seen how Don Pedro Margarite, when reproached by the council for not restraining the license of his soldiery, ignominiously threw down his command and sailed for home. Scarcely less important was the report carried home by Father Boyle, whose access to the spiritual advisers of the king and queen gave him peculiar facilities for poisoning the royal minds. Thus it was that complaints of every kind found ears that welcomed them. Herrera assures us concerning Don Margarite and Father Boyle that "being come to the court, they gave an account that there was no gold in the Indies, and that all the Admiral said was mere sham and banter."

The complaints at length became so numerous and so circumstantial that the monarchs felt obliged to institute a formal and responsible inquiry. The officer chosen for this service was Don John Agnado, a groom of the bedchamber, who had accompanied

Columbus on his first voyage, and had acquitted himself with so much credit that the Admiral had especially recommended his promotion. The appointment was apparently an excellent one, and one that would commend itself to the favour of Columbus. Agnado, armed with credentials giving him ample authority, took four ships laden with provisions and sailed for the colonies, where he arrived in October, 1495.

When the commissioner reached Hispaniola, he found that the Admiral was engaged in his campaign against the brothers of Caonabo. The garrison at Isabella was in charge of the Adelantado. Don Agnado at once made known his extraordinary power and authority by reproving some of the ministers and seizing others. After showing that he had no respect for the authority of Don Bartholomew, he put himself at the head of a troop of horse and foot, and began an advance into the interior for the purpose of going to the Admiral. This course had the natural effect on the garrison and on the islanders. The supposition became general that a new governor had been appointed, and that he was about to seize his predecessor and perhaps even put him to death. The smothered discontents now burst forth into flames. Those who fancied themselves aggrieved by the rigour of the Admiral's rule, those who had found the life of adventure only a life of hardship, those who complained either of the wars or of the tribute, all the malcontents of every race and kind, now hastened to greet the new governor and to denounce the old.

It was immediately evident that the authority of
Columbus was in peril. On learning of the arrival of
Don Agnado, he determined to return to Isabella, and
there welcome the commissioner with the formality
that was due to his royal errand. Accordingly, he
received the letter of their Royal Highnesses with the
sound of trumpets and with the greatest solemnity.
But all this ceremony only seemed to add to the force
of the commission itself. The authority of Don
Agnado was vouched for by the following letter of the
king and queen : —

"Cavaliers, esquires, and other persons who by our
command are in the Indies: We send you thither Juan
Agnado, our Gentleman of the Chamber, who will speak
to you on our part. We command that you give him faith
and credence."

The manner in which Agnado began to pursue his
inquiries must have convinced Columbus that the tide
of his fortune was turning. It became evident that
the reports of Margarite and Boyle had poisoned public opinion about the court. The inquiries, moreover, produced a disquieting effect upon the natives.
A number of caciques met at the headquarters of one
of them, and determined to formulate their complaints
of the Admiral and to pledge their loyalty to his successor. Columbus knew well that these facts would
be duly reported by the commissioner. He determined, therefore, at once to return to Spain, in order
to represent his own cause at court.

There was another reason why Columbus desired to
appear before the sovereigns. By the royal charter

given before the first voyage, he was to be viceroy of all the lands he might discover, and was to have control of all matters of trade and immigration. But now Fonseca had violated this provision of the charter, by giving a number of licenses to private adventurers to trade in the new countries, independently of the Admiral. Columbus saw the evil that was impending, and desired to protest against the issue of such licenses.

The Admiral's departure, however, was delayed by one of those terrible hurricanes which sometimes sweep across the West Indies. The four vessels brought by Don Agnado sank in the harbour, and there were remaining only the two caravels belonging to the Admiral. There was some further delay, moreover, by the report that rich gold mines had been discovered near the southern coast. Investigations seemed to authenticate the report. The Admiral thought it best to establish a strong post in the vicinity of the mine, and so a fort was built which received the name of Saint Christopher.

In the course of the winter months the other forts were put in a condition to make a strong resistance in case of revolt during the Admiral's absence. It was the 10th of March, 1496, before he was ready to sail. The Adelantado was left in command at Isabella. The Admiral sailed on board the "Nina," while Agnado took passage on the other caravel. More than two hundred of the colonists returned with the Admiral, — some of them broken in health, some of them merely sick at heart.

The voyage was one of numerous delays. A few days were spent in coasting along the Caribbean islands; but even after they were well at sea, contrary winds prevailed and very slow progress was made. Provisions finally ran so low that they had to be doled out in pittances, and it is said that all the Admiral's authority was needed to prevent the ship's company from killing and eating the Carib prisoners who were on board. It was only after a voyage of three months' duration that the ships put into the Bay of Cadiz on the 11th of June, 1496.

CHAPTER V.

THE THIRD VOYAGE.

THE circumstances attending the disembarking of Columbus on his return after the second voyage were of a nature to emphasize rather than allay the popular opinion that had been aroused against him. Three years before, the expedition had gone out with the most joyous anticipations. Representatives of noble and gentle families had begged the privilege of going in the hope of easily finding either renown or fortune. All these expectations had been disappointed. A large proportion of those who had gone out had lost their lives; many others remained to battle still longer with poverty, and perhaps even with hunger; while the two hundred or more wretched creatures who now "crawled out of the ships" told their tales of disastrous experience to the eyes as well as to the ears of the people. It is related that Columbus himself was unshaven, and that he was clad with the robe and girdled with the cord of the Franciscans.

On arriving at the port of Cadiz, the Admiral found three caravels on the point of sailing with provisions for the colony. Seeking an interview with the commander, he learned much in regard to the state of feeling that awaited him.   In view of this information, he wrote a letter to thē Adelantado, not only to apprise him of his own safe arrival, but also to urge him to endeavour by every possible means to bring the island into a peaceful and productive condition.   He urged his brother to appease all discontents and commotions, and to use the utmost diligence in exploring and working the mines that had recently been discovered.

As soon as tidings of his arrival reached the sovereigns, they sent Columbus a letter congratulating him on his safe return, and inviting him to court. Accordingly, he at once made all necessary preparations to go to Almazan, where the court was at that time established.   Desiring to keep alive an interest in his discoveries, he made a studious display of the curiosities and treasures he had brought with him. As at the end of the first voyage, the people along the way showed great interest in the natives and in the products of the new islands.

The king and queen, though temporarily absent, soon returned to Almazan, and gave him a gracious reception.   It was evident that however much of adverse criticism they may have heard, they were disposed to hold in strict reserve any questionings they may have had in regard to the general wisdom of his administrative methods.

Columbus gave a full account of his explorations in Cuba, and dwelt in detail upon the promises held forth by the gold mines recently discovered.   If we may judge from its immediate consequences, we must infer that the report made a favourable and deep impression.

The sovereigns even went so far as to give special and exceptional evidence of their approval. In April of 1497 they confirmed anew the commissions and hereditary privileges granted before the first voyage; they confirmed and even made hereditary the appointment of Bartholomew Columbus to the office of Adelantado, which at first had been criticised as an undue exercise of authority by the Admiral; they promised to comply with his request for eight ships with which to complete his explorations and annex the mainland to their dominions. A little later the queen also appointed his son Fernando as a page.

Other favours of a less personal nature were also freely granted. It was determined that there should be sent out on the new fleet three hundred and thirty men in the pay of the sovereigns. Others might be enlisted by the Admiral, on condition that their pay could be provided for in some other way. Those who volunteered to go without pay were to receive a third part of the gold they might get out of the mines, and nine tenths of all other products. The residue in both cases was to be turned over to the royal officers. The Admiral also obtained the privilege of transporting all criminals to the Indies, to serve there for a number of years. This exceedingly unwise and unfortunate provision, putting, as it did, the stamp of ignominy upon service in the colony, exerted a pernicious influence, not only in preventing enlistments, but also in demoralizing future life in the colonies.

These favours and promises by the sovereigns were more than Columbus had dared even to hope for. But notwithstanding the kind, if not the enthusiastic, favour of the sovereigns, the promises were not speedily to be fulfilled. There were several reasons why the furnishing of the ships was a matter of most annoying delay. During the long months of waiting, Columbus was under the roof of Andres Bernaldez, who turned to account many of his interviews with the Admiral in his History of the Spanish Kings. Columbus left with Bernaldez several important documents which the historian made the basis of much of his History. It is from Bernaldez that we get the most definite account of the temper and opposition of the people, as well as the grounds of their discontent. The whole may be expressed in the single word " disappointment." The cost of the expeditions had been very great, and the returns very small. A tradition has assumed the form of a popular belief that the gold brought back to Spain by this second expedition was so abundant that it was used to ornament palaces and gild cathedrals. But this belief must be discarded; for we learn from Bernaldez that the gold brought back consisted mainly of personal ornaments.

There were several causes for delay in fitting out the third expedition. Spain was now at war with France in regard to that vexed question which involved the suzerainty of Naples. Besides a powerful army in Italy under Gonzalo de Cordova, Spain was obliged to keep an army on her own frontier, which was threatened with an invasion from France. A

strong fleet had to be kept in the Mediterranean, and
another was called for to defend the Atlantic coasts
of the Spanish peninsula. But even these were not
all. Ferdinand and Isabella, if not far-seeing, were
far-reaching in their ambition to extend their international importance by judicious matrimonial alliances
of their children. This was to be done, not simply
by the marriage of Catherine of Aragon with Prince
Henry of England, but also by the far more important
double alliance with Austria. The arrangements for
the Austrian nuptials were now complete, and a mag-
nificent armada of a hundred and twenty ships, with
twenty thousand persons on board, had been sent as a
convoy of the Princess Juana to Flanders, where she
was to marry Philip, the archduke of Austria, and
bring back the Austrian Princess Margarita, who was
to complete the double Austrian alliance by marrying
Prince Juan.

These several demands quite exhausted the maritime resources of the Spanish Government. Delay
therefore in the equipment of ships for the third
expedition of Columbus was inevitable. But there
were also other reasons that emphasized and reinforced the same tendencies. The affairs of the Indian Office, after once having been sequestered, had
now been restored to the control of Fonseca. For a
time they had been transferred to the direction of
Antonio de Torres; but in consequence of high and
unreasonable demands, he had been removed from
office, and Fonseca, the Bishop of Badajoz, had been
reinstated. Fonseca had never been actively helpful

to Columbus, and as time had passed on, what at first had an air of indifference, gradually changed to ill-concealed enmity. In the position to which he had now been reinstated it was easy for him to impede, if not frustrate, all the navigator's plans. The delay became intolerable. In the spring of 1498, Columbus, after nearly two years had elapsed since his second return, presented a direct appeal to the queen, making urgent representations of the misery to which the colonists had been reduced. The appeal was successful; two ships with supplies for the colony were despatched early in February, 1498.

The fitting-out of the vessels that were to be commanded by Columbus himself was retarded by many very annoying conditions. Fonseca seemed determined to throw every obstacle in his way. It was everywhere evident, moreover, that the popular favour in which the Admiral had been more or less generally held was fast slipping away. At one time he thought of abandoning the enterprise altogether; and in one of his letters he intimates that he was restrained from doing so only by his unwillingness to disoblige or disappoint the queen.

Of the various annoyances that occurred, there were two that are worthy of note. The sovereigns ordered six million maravedis to be set apart for the equipment of the new expedition. But soon after the arrival of the three caravels of slaves in the autumn of 1495, word was circulated that the fleet was freighted with *bars of gold*. The report had so much influence on the sovereigns that they revoked

their order for six million maravedis, and directed
that the necessary money for the new expedition
should be taken from the gold brought home. What
was the chagrin of Columbus and of all his friends
to find that what was only a wretched joke of one
of the ship's commanders had been taken in serious earnest even by Ferdinand and Isabella. When
the truth came to be known, it was found that the
bars of gold were only slaves kept behind bars, with
the design of converting them into gold in the
market of Seville. It is not difficult to imagine the
indignation of Isabella when the truth came to be
known. The other affair alluded to was the personal altercation that occurred between Columbus
and Breviesca, the treasurer of Fonseca. The very
day when the squadron was about to embark, Columbus was assailed in so insolent a manner by this official that he lost his self-control, and not only struck
his accuser to the ground, but kicked him in his
paroxysm of rage. As to the extent of the provocation, Las Casas, who relates the anecdote, leaves us
in doubt; but the influence of such a spectacle could
hardly have been favourable to the Admiral.

It was the 30th day of May, 1498, before the expedition was ready to sail. The fleet, consisting of six
ships loaded with provisions and other necessaries for
the planters in Hispaniola, was detained at the Canary and Cape de Verde islands until the 5th of July.
From the island of Ferro Columbus decided to send
three of the vessels to Hispaniola, and to sail in a more
southerly direction with the rest, for the purpose of

12

making further discoveries. He designed to make the course southwest until they should reach the equinoctial line, and then to take a course due west. But the currents flowed so strongly toward the north, and the heat was so severe, that this purpose was abandoned before they reached the equator. Fernando, with characteristic exaggeration, says that "had it not rained sometimes, and the sun been clouded, he thought they would have been burned alive, together with the ships, for the heat was so violent that nothing could withstand it." Las Casas, who had other sources of authentic information besides the narrative of Columbus, declares that but for this heat and the fact that the vessels were becalmed eight days, the Admiral would have taken a course so far to the south that the fleet would have been carried to the coast of Brazil. Be this as it may, the effect of the temperature on the men and on the provisions was such that on the last day of July the Admiral, thinking they were now south of the Caribbean islands, resolved to abandon their course and make for Hispaniola. Sailing toward the northwest one day, the man at the lookout descried land to the westward, which, because of the three mountains that arose above the horizon, Columbus called Trinidad. This discovery led to a little delay. Cruising about the island for a considerable time without finding a harbour, he came to deep soundings near Point Alcatraz, where he decided to take in water and make such repairs as the shrinkage of the timbers had made necessary. From the point where they now were, the low lands about the mouth

of the Orinoco were plainly visible; and the incident is memorable because, notwithstanding the assertion of Oviedo that Vespucius anticipated Columbus
in reaching the mainland, it was probably here that
the Spaniards obtained the first sight of the western
continent. It was on the 1st day of August, 1498, —
two months and ten days after Vasco da Gama had
cast anchor in the bay of Calicut.

After necessary delays the little fleet resumed its
westerly course. Although in his letter to the Spanish court, the Admiral gives a graphic account of
the rush of waters from the Orinoco, he seems not
at first to have suspected that he was in sight of
the mainland. The waters delivered to the ocean
by this river came with such impetuous force that
they seemed to produce a ridge along the top of
which the squadron was borne at a furious rate into the
Gulf of Paria. "Even to-day," wrote Columbus, "I
shudder lest the waters should have upset the vessel
when they came under its bows." We now know
that the tumult of the waters was very largely the
result of the African current wedging in between
the island of Trinidad and the mainland, and forming that stupendous flow which on emerging from the
Caribbean Sea is known as the Gulf Stream.

In sailing along the coast the Admiral met with
nothing but friendly treatment from the natives.
The region at the left of the Gulf of Paria he called
Gracia. At length the immense volume of waters
passing through the mouths of the Orinoco led him
to surmise that the land he had been calling an island

was in fact the continent. Holding this conjecture with increasing confidence, he was unwilling to give any considerable time to further exploration; and accordingly, after passing through what he called the Boca del Drago, or Dragon's Mouth, he sailed directly for Hispaniola. His departure was hastened by the desire, not only of landing the stores he had in charge, but also of learning the truth in regard to the reports of disturbance among the colonists that had reached Spain before his embarkation.

Before following him, however, to the unhappy colony, it may not be out of place to make note of a few of his reflections, as recorded in his own words. There is nothing in the life of Columbus more interesting than his letter to the court describing this third voyage, and commenting on the various phenomena which he observed. The minute and ingenious details of this letter not only show how easily he was captivated by delusions, but they also throw a flood of light on his general habit of mind. It is impossible to quote the letter at length, but a few of his conclusions may not be omitted.

In remarking that Ptolemy and all the other ancient writers regarded the earth as spherical, he says that they had had no opportunity of observing the region he was now exploring, and that in consequence they had fallen into error. To his mind it was clear that the form of the earth was not globular, but pear-shaped, and that the form of a pear about the stem was the form of the earth in the region he had discovered. He had at all times noted a marked change in the temperature on crossing the one hundredth meridian. The north star also perceptibly changed its relative position in regard to the horizon at this point. The deflection of the needle here changed from five degrees to the east to as many degrees to the west. The waters of the great river flowing into the Gulf of Paria could hardly come with a tumultuous volume for any other reason. As they sailed away from this region, they were so rapidly descending that they easily made sixty-five leagues in a day, which they could hardly have done on an ascending or a level sea.

It was his opinion, moreover, derived from numerous considerations, that the point at the stem of the pear represented the garden of Paradise. "I do not suppose," he writes, "that the earthly Paradise is in the form of a rugged mountain, as the descriptions of it have made it appear, but that it is on the summit of the spot which I have described as being in the form of the neck of a pear. The approach to it from a distance must be by a constant and gradual ascent; but I believe that, as I have already said, no one could ever reach the top. I think also that the water I have described may proceed from it, though it be far off, and that stopping at the place I have just left, it forms this lake." He further states: "There are great indications of this being the terrestrial paradise, for its site coincides with the opinion of the holy and wise theologians whom I have mentioned."

The speculations of Columbus in regard to the currents of the ocean and their effects on the shape of the islands are interesting; but they are important only as revealing the observing and generalizing habit of his mind. His remarks on the characteristics of the natives are more important. Their superior intelligence and courage, as well as their lighter colour, and even their long, smooth hair, he attributes to the mildness of the climate, occasioned by the altitude of this portion of the pear-shaped earth.

Resuming the general course of his voyage toward the northwest, after pausing for a time at Margarita he arrived at the harbour of San Domingo on the 30th of August, 1798.

In order to understand the condition of affairs on the arrival of the Admiral, it is necessary to call attention briefly to the history of the island during the two years of his absence.

We find that early in the administration of the Adelantado he sent to Spain three hundred slaves from Hispaniola. As these were represented as having been taken while they were killing Christians, this disposition of them seems not to have met with any insurmountable disfavour. Indeed, the sovereigns had given orders that all those who should be found guilty should be sent to Spain. The way was thus opened for an iniquitous traffic by a royal order that simply provided for an inevitable flexibility of interpretation under an imperfect administration of justice. There was no reason to anticipate that there would in the future be any insurmountable obstacle to a profitable exercise of the trade in slaves. Human nature, as it revealed itself in the fifteenth century, might well be trusted to find the means.

The order, already alluded to, authorizing judges to transport criminals to the Indies, had already begun to exert its baleful influence ; and a still more pernicious result came from the further edict giving an indulgence to such criminals as should go out at their own expense and serve under the Admiral. The provisions of this edict, which must have been recommended by Columbus himself, could hardly have been more ingeniously framed for the purpose of bringing the greatest harm to the colony. They not only made all labour disreputable, but they drew into the colonies the worst classes of criminals. Those to whom an indulgence was most desirable, were the very men who had committed the most flagrant crimes ; and these were the persons that most eagerly accepted the opportunity. Three years later, when Columbus was under accusation, he excused the acts complained of by referring to the badness of the men who were allowed to go out under this edict ; but he did not call attention to the fact that the edict was one which he himself had recommended. Of these he said, with unwonted emphasis : "I swear that numbers of men have gone to the Indies who did not deserve water from God or man." The colony as made up in 1493 was not of a nature to bear with impunity such an influx of rascality.

Another royal order that contributed not a little to the future turbulence of the islands was the one which provided for what are known as the *repartimientos*. This edict was also issued in 1497, and it authorized the Admiral to give in the most formal way any of the lands discovered to any Spaniard, with all rights "to hold, to sell, to traffic with, and to alienate and to do with it and in it all that he likes or may think good."

Here, then, was introduced an ingenious instrument of interminable discord. The ill effects of these several edicts were not mitigated by the methods of government pursued by the Adelantado; but, on the contrary, Don Bartholomew was so unwise as to contribute in many ways to the prevailing dissatisfaction and turbulence.

Before the Admiral had sailed for home, as we have already seen, gold mines had been discovered near the southern coast of the island. He had promptly reported the discovery and had recommended the opening of the mines and the establishment of a port at no remote distance. The recommendations were favorably received by the monarchs, and the captain of the fleet which Columbus met as he was entering the bay of Cadiz was the bearer of the letter of approval. The Admiral, on receiving this letter, at once wrote to his brother, ordering him to begin work at once to carry out the royal pleasure in regard to the mines and the establishment of a port on the southern coast of the island. He also directed him to spare no pains to conciliate all the adverse interests and bind them into harmonious unity of purpose.

Don Bartholomew on receiving this letter at once proceeded southward and fixed upon the mouth of the river Ozama as the site of the new port. Send-

ing for artisans and labourers, he at once began the
building of a fortress which he named San Domingo,
and which afterward gave its name to the chief port
and city of the island. The purpose of the Admiral
and of his brother seems to have been ultimately to
abandon Isabella and to establish in the new town on
the southern coast the seat of government of the
colony. In accordance with this design, Don Bartholomew planned to transport to the southern coast
all of the working population at Isabella excepting
so many as were necessary to complete the two caravels now in process of construction.

Scarcely was the building of the new port and
town fairly undertaken when the Adelantado became
involved in what seems to have been a most needless
and disastrous undertaking. No one of the early
authorities gives any justifiable reason for the enterprise. The brief statement of Herrera has the advantage of clearness, and is perhaps as trustworthy
as any other. His language is: "The work having
begun, Don Bartholomew resolved to view the kingdom of Behechio, called Xaragua, of whose state
and government and of whose sister Anacaona he
had heard so much talk." That this intimation concerning Anacaona is not altogether gratuitous may be
inferred from numerous statements in the original
authorities. Fernando Columbus, in explaining why
his uncle wished to establish himself in Xaragua,
gives several reasons touching climate, soil, etc., and
then adds: " But above all, because the women were
the handsomest and of the most pleasing conversa-

tion of any." It is a deplorable fact, but one that can hardly be ignored, that the motives here ascribed to Don Bartholomew were a constant element, not only of distrust and hatred in all the relations of the Spaniards with the natives, but also a constant element of danger and depletion.[4]

The expedition into Xaragua — a province situated in the western portion of the island — was fraught with many new complications. The cacique Behechio at first seemed disposed to offer a spirited and warlike resistance. But on receiving the assurance that the mission was a friendly one, for the purpose of paying respect to himself and his sister, he adopted the policy of welcoming the Adelantado in the most friendly manner. Don Bartholomew, with his soldiers, was thus admitted to the very heart of the kingdom. It was now easy for him to complete his errand by imposing tribute. Behechio answered that tribute would be impossible, as there was no gold within his kingdom ; whereupon the lieutenant declared that he would be content to receive tribute in the products of the territory. On these conditions and in this manner it was that the suzerainty of the Spaniards was established over the western portion of the island.

[1] Fernando Columbus, in describing the condition of the colony on the return of the Admiral, says . " Perciocchè gran parte della gente, da lui lasciatavi, era già morta, e degli altri ve n' erano piu di cento sessanta ammalati di mal Francese " (Vita di Christoforo Colombo, descritta da Ferdinando, suo figlio, Londra, 1867, cap. lxxiii. p. 239).

On returning to Isabella, Don Bartholomew had found a deplorable state of affairs. During his absence more than three hundred of the colonists had died of various diseases. Among the living, moreover, discontents were universal. He distributed the sick among the various forts and friendly Indian villages in the vicinity, and then set out for San Domingo, collecting tribute by the way. In all these energetic proceedings he constantly augmented the accumulations of ill-will, not only on the part of the Spaniards, but also on that of the natives. The islanders needed only an occasion and a leader to ignite them into a general conflagration; and neither was long wanting. The authorities do not quite agree as to the exact time when the outburst took place; but the matter of a precise date is not important. Of the fact itself there seems no room for doubt.

There was everywhere complaint on the part of the natives of the tribute imposed upon them; and nothing but the hopelessness of the situation had prevented them so long from a general attempt to throw off their hateful yoke. On the occasion of this last tribute several of the minor chiefs complained to the cacique Guarionex, and urged a general rising of the Indians. This cacique was greatly respected for his intelligence, as well as for his prudence and his courage. Though well aware of the power of the Spaniards, he finally consented to put himself at the head of a general revolt. A battle ensued, in which the Spaniards, as usual, were successful, taking Guarionex and many other important persons captive. The Adelantado ordered the movers in the insurrection to be put to death; but he thought it politic and prudent to deliver Guarionex up to his people.

Having thus settled the revolt in the centre of the island, and hearing that the tribute of Behechio was ready for him, Don Bartholomew left the region between Isabella and San Domingo in the control of his brother Diego, and took his departure for the west to visit Xaragua. But the occasion of his going was the signal for further revolt. Now, however, he had to confront an insurrection, not of the Indians, but of the Spaniards themselves.

Before the Admiral had left Hispaniola for Spain in 1496, he appointed Francis Roldan chief justice of the island. This officer was endowed with an arrogant and turbulent temper, and it soon became apparent that there were abundant causes of friction between him and the Adelantado. Disagreement between the executive and judicial authorities is always more or less liable to occur in primitive governments; and although the chief authority must have been in the hands of the governor, it is probable that their functions were never very clearly defined. Roldan early began to show signs of a restive spirit, which waxed stronger and stronger until it broke forth into open defiance. By a watchful seizing of opportunities for encouraging the complaints of the people, and by ingeniously declaring how the methods of rule ought to be modified, he had no difficulty in attaching to him a formidable party. The absence of Don

Bartholomew and the weakness of Don Diego now afforded him an opportunity. Fernando Columbus gives details of Roldan's plan to assassinate the Adelantado and then make himself master of the island. He was to await the return of Don Bartholomew to Isabella, and then, having put him to death, was to proclaim himself chief ruler of the island. The Adelantado, however, received tidings of the insurrection before reaching Isabella, and so put himself on his guard. But no effort to bring Roldan to terms was successful. The leader of the rebellion had secured a numerous following, both of natives and of Spaniards; and the consequence was that for months the island was kept in such turbulence that no progress could be made either in working the mines or in building the new city.

The two vessels which the Admiral sent out with provisions arrived in the spring of 1498. The same ships brought the royal commission confirming the appointment of Don Bartholomew as Adelantado, or Lord Lieutenant, of the islands, and conveying the further information that the Admiral himself, with a fleet of six ships, was soon to embark for the same destination. The commission was duly proclaimed, and on the strength of this confirmation of authority and the prospect of the speedy arrival of the Admiral, a new effort was made to bring Roldan to terms. But even this attempt was not successful. After ravaging considerable portions of the centre of the island, Roldan entered with his followers into the luxuriant regions of Xaragua, there to await coming events. Though Roldan was not subdued, it is probable that the arrival of reinforcements saved the government of Don Bartholomew from complete destruction.

In midsummer the three ships despatched by Columbus from the Canaries with provisions arrived off the south coast of the island. Ignorant of the situation of San Domingo, and carried by strong winds and currents in a westerly direction, they made their landing, as if adverse fates were in control, in the very territory held by Roldan. As if to give added significance to this misfortune, the captains decided that the labouring-men should go ashore, and make their way on foot to San Domingo. The result was that, according to Herrera, Roldan " easily persuaded them to stay with him, telling them at the same time how they would live with him, which was only going about from one town to another, taking the gold and what else they saw fit."

Such was the condition of affairs when Christopher Columbus arrived on the 22d of August, 1498. It was not until some days later that the three caravels with supplies, after returning from Xaragua, reached the same port. In one of his letters, written a year later, Columbus says : " I found nearly half the colonists of Hispaniola in a state of revolt."

The formidable extent of this insurrection is revealed, not only by the numbers that participated in it, but also by the spirit shown by those in revolt, as well as by those in authority. Neither Don Bartholomew nor the Admiral thought it prudent to move against Roldan and attempt to crush him by force. This hesitating prudence can only be explained by the fear that such a movement would weaken rather than strengthen the colony; and such a fear could be justified only by a very wide-spread and deep-seated spirit of dissatisfaction. Columbus evidently expected on his arrival to find that the revolt of Roldan had its root in a personal antipathy to the Adelantado, and that as soon as he should himself resume direct control of affairs, all discontent would subside. But in this he was bitterly disappointed. The Alcalde continued to maintain an attitude of stubborn defiance. Negotiations were entered into from time to time; but they proceeded slowly, and only served to show the extent and the spirit of the party in revolt.

It was while these perplexing events were taking place that Columbus sent back to Spain such of the ships as were not needed in the colonies.

In November of 1498 an elaborate agreement was reached, the details of which reveal at once the weakness of Columbus and the strength of Roldan. It had all the characteristics of a treaty, in which every concession, except that of abandoning the island to the rebellion, was made by the Admiral. Columbus agreed to furnish within fifty days two vessels for transporting the rebels to Spain, to furnish them with ample provisions for the voyage, to allow one slave, man or woman, to each of Roldan's men, to pledge his honour as a Spanish gentleman that he would do nothing to detain or obstruct the vessels, and to write to the sovereigns a letter designed to absolve Roldan and his men from all blame.

But even this treaty, duly signed and sealed on the 21st of November, did not bring this painful history to an end. The vessels were not ready in time. It was the midsummer of the following year before Columbus had put the ships at the disposal of Roldan and his men. This may not have been the fault of the Admiral, but it furnished a least a pretext for abandoning the contract on the part of Roldan. His men seem to have been unwilling to return to the restraints of civilization, and it was necessary to begin negotiations on another basis. The settlement finally agreed upon and signed on the 5th of November, 1499, contained the four following provisions: First, that fifteen of Roldan's men should be sent to Spain in the first vessel that went; secondly, that to those that remained, Columbus should give land and houses for their pay; thirdly, that proclamation should be made that all that had happened had resulted from false reports and through the fault of bad men; and fourthly, that Columbus should now appoint Roldan perpetual judge. The conditions of this agreement were fulfilled, and thus, after Columbus had put forth efforts extending over nearly a year and a half, the rebellion was brought to an end by a treaty that is a sad commentary on the condition of affairs in the island.

But quiet was not yet by any means to be restored. No sooner was Roldan's rebellion suppressed than the appearance of another turbulent spirit on the scene threatened to make the permanent establishment of peace impossible. Alonzo de Ojeda, soon after his treacherous exploit in the capture of the cacique Caonabo, had been despatched with four vessels on a voyage of exploration. With the details of his expedition, however interesting in themselves, we have nothing in this connection to do, except to note the fact that he returned to Hispaniola just after matters had been adjusted between Columbus and Roldan. However Ojeda may have felt toward his chief at the time of his departure, it is evident that he brought back from his voyage a malignant enmity. He was a strong partisan of Fonseca, and he now represented that the queen was at the point of death, that her demise would deprive Columbus of his last friend, and that it would not be difficult so to arrange matters that Columbus would soon be stripped of his authority. To the honour of Roldan it must be said that he not only opposed a stern resistance to all Ojeda's schemes, but that he acted with strict loyalty to the interests of Columbus. Nevertheless, for months the island was kept in turmoil, the forces of Roldan were pitted against those of Ojeda, and it was not until after several hostile skirmishes that the hopes of this new rebel were finally dispelled.

Meanwhile reports of the unhappy situation were finding their way back to Spain. Ojeda lost no opportunity to write to Fonseca and to pour the poison of his representations into the mind of the minister. Don Fernando tells us that during the period of these disorders " many of the rebels sent letters from Hispaniola, and others, when returned to Spain, did not cease to give false information to the king and his council against the Admiral and his brother."

It was while these various occurrences were taking place that Columbus sent back to Spain five of the vessels that had set out with him on his third voyage. The freightage and the news borne by the ships were most unfortunate for the cause of the Admiral. The caravels were laden with slaves for the Spanish market. Such a method of recruiting the colonial treasury was not indeed unknown, for slaves had already before been sent back and sold for the benefit of the expedition. But hitherto the Indian slave-trade had been kept within the domain of custom and ecclesiastical sanction. In the fifteenth century infidels taken in war were thrown upon the slave-market without provoking ecclesiastical protest. In the war against the Moors the victors often sold prisoners in large numbers, and even the sensibilities of Isabella seem not to have been offended by such a proceeding. But the Indians now to be sent to the auction-block had been taken in a very different way. Many of the native men and women had found the tribute of service demanded of them so oppressive or revolting that they had fled to the forests as a means of escape. But in this dash for liberty they were pursued, and often overtaken. Those who were captured were thrown into the ships and held in close confinement until the time of sailing. It is painful to relate that Columbus not only sanctioned and directed this proceeding, but that in his letter to the sovereigns he even entered into an account of the pecuniary advantage that would arise from these slave-dealing transactions. He estimated that as many slaves could be furnished as the Spanish market would demand, and that from this species of traffic a revenue of as much as forty million maravedis might be derived. Not only this, but he even alludes to the intended adoption on the part of private individuals of a system of exchange of slaves for goods wanted in colonial life. According to this scheme, as outlined by the Admiral, the colonists were to furnish slaves to the shipowners who were to take this human freightage to Spain, and then, having disposed of it and taken their commission, invest the remaining proceeds in the articles needed, and carry them back to the traders in the islands. The plan had all the cold-hearted brutality of a practised slave-dealer.

The misfortune of this policy to Columbus was in the relation of the king and queen respectively to the colonial enterprise. Ferdinand had never shown himself heartily favourable to the projects of the Admiral. The queen, on the other hand, had taken a much larger and juster view of the importance and glory of the discovery. But Isabella had from the first been extremely sensitive on the matter of reducing the native Indians to a condition of slavery. Before she would consent to the sale of a former consignment, she had required that proofs should be furnished of their having been taken in open warfare, and also that an ecclesiastical commission should certify to the regularity and propriety of such a proceeding.

These requirements, if no other, should have prevented Columbus from presuming very much upon
any indulgent leniency on this subject.   In view of
the queen's previous attitude in regard to the matter
of slavery, no intelligent observer can think it strange
that the course Columbus was now taking gave great
offence, if it did not arouse an earnest indignation.

It is evident, moreover, that the scruples of the
queen in regard to the general wisdom of Columbus's
course must have received new significance from
the news that came from the island.   It is true that
Columbus himself wrote an elaborate account of the
causes of the revolt; but it is also true that the same
ships that carried the slaves and the report of the
Admiral, carried also several descriptions of affairs
by Roldan and his followers.   The Admiral and the
Lord Lieutenant were freely charged with every species of enormity.   Nor were these charges confined
to generalities.   The rebels went so far as to declare
that the tyranny of the rule in the islands was so intolerable that nothing but revolt was possible.   They
also very adroitly called attention to the fact that notwithstanding all the reports that received currency in
regard to the discoveries of gold, no gold of any
amount had as yet found its way back to Spain.

Besides these reports, numerous others of a more
private nature were sent by colonists to their friends
at home, all of them laden with gloom and dissatisfaction.   That the administrations of the Admiral
and the Lord Lieutenant were very unpopular, there
can be no doubt whatever in the mind of any one

who reads the original accounts; and these expressions of popular disfavour streamed back to the mother-country by every means of conveyance. Nor did these tidings fall upon unwelcoming ears. Those who had sent out friends only to hear of their death or misfortunes; those who were filled with envy at the success of one whom they regarded as merely a foreign adventurer; those who were embittered by disappointment that no pecuniary returns had been received, — all these and thousands of others now united in one general cry of denunciation. The Admiral's son Fernando gives a vivid picture of the complaints made against his father. Columbus himself, in writing to the nurse of Prince Juan at this period, said : " I have now reached a point where there is no man so vile but thinks it his right to insult me. . . . If I had plundered the Indies, even to the country where is the fabled altar of St. Peter's, and had given them all to the Moors, they could not have shown toward me more bitter enmity than they have done in Spain."

That much of this unpopularity was unjust and unreasonable, there can be no doubt whatever. But even when we have conceded this, there still remains the great fact of a popular outcry; and such an outcry always justifies at least an inquiry. It must not, therefore, be regarded as strange that the Spanish sovereigns at length decided to make an official investigation. Indeed, any other course would have been little less than a culpable disregard of a powerful public sentiment.

Such were the influences that were borne in upon

the king and queen.   There is evidence that soon
after the return of the five vessels with their cargo of
slaves, Ferdinand and Isabella began to take into consideration the question of suspending the Admiral.
They did not, however, act in haste.   The ships arrived with their ill-omened freightage in November of
1498.   In the course of the following winter the monarchs decided definitively that an investigation should
be made.   On the 21st of March, 1499, they issued
a commission authorizing Francis de Bobadilla " to
ascertain what persons have raised themselves against
justice in the island of Hispaniola, and to proceed
against them according to law."

Bobadilla was an officer of the royal household
and a commander of one of the military and religious
orders.   His general reputation was good.   Oviedo
says that he was " a very honest and religious man."
The misfortune of the appointment was not so much
in the badness of the man as in the badness of the
situation in which he was placed.   The instructions
given by Ferdinand and Isabella have been preserved ; and as we read them we cannot escape the
conviction that they subjected Bobadilla to a temptation greater than ordinary human nature could bear.
He received a series of commissions, each conferring
greater authority than that conferred by the one before, each intended to be used only in case of imperative emergency.   In one of these commissions
Bobadilla was authorized to issue his commands in
the royal name and to send back to Spain " any cavaliers or other persons," in case he should think such a

course necessary for the service. Another commission authorizes Bobadilla to require Columbus to surrender " the fortresses, ships, houses, arms, ammunition, cattle, and all other royal property, under penalty of the customary punishment for disobedience of a royal order."

Having received these general instructions, Bobadilla was made the bearer of the following letter to the Admiral : —

DON CHRISTOPHER COLUMBUS, *our Admiral of the Ocean :*

We have commanded the commendador, Francis de Bobadilla, the bearer of this, that he speak to you on our part some things which he will tell you. We pray you give him faith and credence, and act accordingly.

But notwithstanding this authority, for some reason that has not been adequately explained, Bobadilla was not despatched to the Indies until a year from the following July. It is very easy to conjecture that the sovereigns were more than willing that, if possible, Columbus should still work out the problem for himself. They may have desired Bobadilla to try his influence at first from a distance, in the hope that extreme measures might not have to be resorted to. But this purpose seems not to have been successful. If we accept of this explanation of the delay, we can hardly withhold from the sovereigns some measure of commendation for their caution and prudence.

But caution and prudence formed no part of the

policy pursued after Bobadilla was sent to Hispaniola.
It is difficult to believe that the commissioner acted
without at least the royal approval of a policy of vigour, though it is impossible to suppose that the sovereigns would have given their sanction in detail to the
manner in which he performed his mission. Bobadilla
seems at least not to have been unwilling to act with
energy and directness. There is no evidence that he
was not high-principled, or that he was actuated by
any other motives than those of the public good ; but
he was a person of strong prejudices and of narrow-
ness of mind, and consequently he was unable to
distinguish between vigour and coarse brutality.

The arrival of Bobadilla at San Domingo was on
the 23d of August, 1499. He found affairs in extreme disorder. The first information he received
was that seven of the rebels had just been hanged,
and that five more had been condemned and were
awaiting a similar fate. Las Casas tells us that as
Bobadilla entered the river, he beheld on either hand
a gibbet, and on it the body of a prominent Spaniard
lately executed ! The impression thus made upon
his mind was no doubt intensified by the rumours
that came from every quarter. He seems to have
regarded what he saw and heard as conclusive evidence of the Admiral's cruelty and culpability.

The next morning, after mass, Bobadilla ordered
the letter authorizing him to make investigations to
be read before the assembled populace about the
church-door. The commission authorized him to
seize persons and fortresses, to sequestrate the prop-

erty of delinquents, and finally called upon the Admiral and all others in authority to assist in the discharge of his duties. The Admiral and the Adelantado were in another part of the island, the command at San Domingo having been intrusted to Don Diego. After the reading of the commission, Bobadilla demanded of the acting governor that he surrender the prisoners that were held for execution, together with the evidence concerning them. The reply was given that the prisoners were held by command of the Admiral, and that the Admiral's authority was superior to any that Bobadilla might possess, and therefore that the prisoners could not be given up. This defiant answer to his demand provoked Bobadilla into bringing forward all the reserves of his authority. Accordingly, on the next morning, as soon as mass was said, he caused his other letter to be proclaimed, investing him with the government of the islands and of the continent. After taking the oath of office, he produced the third letter of the Crown, ordering Columbus to deliver up all the royal property; and then, as if to clinch popular favour, he produced an additional mandate, requiring him, at the earliest practicable moment, to pay all arrears of wages due to persons in the royal service.

This proclamation had the desired effect. The populace, many of whom were suffering from arrears in payment of wages, hailed the new governor as a benefactor and a saviour.

Thus it was that, by a very natural series of events,

the narrow mind of Bobadilla was led on to a pre-
cipitate assumption of all the authority conferred
upon him. He decided to act with an energy that
amounted to brutality. His next step was to take
possession of the Admiral's house, and then, sending
the royal letter, to summon the Admiral before him.
No resistance was offered either by Columbus or by
either of his brothers. Indeed, the authority conferred by the commission and the attitude of the
populace made resistance impossible. Bobadilla,
without hesitation, not only arrested them, but put
them into chains.

No sooner was it apparent that the commissioner
was disposed to act with energy than the whole pack
of malcontents set up their cry of accusation. They
told how Columbus had made them work on the
fortresses and other buildings even when they were
sick; how he had condemned them to be whipped
even for stealing a peck of wheat when they were
dying with hunger; how he had not baptized Indians, because he desired to make slaves rather than
Christians; and, finally, how he had entered into unjust wars with the natives, in order that he might
capture slaves to be sent to the markets in Spain.
Many of these accusations, if the facts could have
been understood, might doubtless have been explained in a way to reflect no discredit upon the
Admiral; they might even have shown proof of his
firmness and sagacity as a ruler. But there was no
opportunity for explanation. It is only certain that
the populace rejoiced in the coming of Bobadilla,

and that they encouraged him in all his acts of violence.

Thus it was that the disaster toward which so many things had been tending was finally consummated. It has been fortunate for the memory of Columbus that the act of suspension was carried out with such total disregard of what the navigator had accomplished. In accordance with a well-known impulse of human nature, the sympathies of all generous minds from that time to this have been enlisted in his favour. These sympathies have often led to a forgetfulness of the grievances under which the colonists were suffering. But in the light of all the facts that are accessible, it is difficult to believe that the sovereigns were wrong in providing for his removal. The only cause of just complaint is the fact that it was not done in a manner that was worthy of his great achievements.

Bobadilla acted with such brutal energy, and the outcries of the poplace were so violent, that Columbus believed his life was to be sacrificed. There is no reason to suppose, however, that Bobadilla ever for a moment thought of bringing the Admiral to execution. He decided at once to send the prisoners to Spain. Alonzo de Villejo was put in charge of the Admiral and of the two brothers. Las Casas says of Villejo: "He was a worthy hidalgo and my particular friend." When the new custodian with his guard entered the prison, Columbus supposed it was to conduct him to the scaffold. Villejo at once reassured him, however, and told him his errand was to transfer him to the ship, and that they were at once to embark for Spain. Columbus may well have felt like one restored from death to life. But as the officers took him to the ship, they were followed by the insulting scoffs of the rabble; for all seemed to take a brutal satisfaction in heaping indignities upon his head.

On shipboard Villejo treated his illustrious prisoner with every consideration. He offered to remove the irons; but to this Columbus would not consent. It is a signifiant indication of his character that he haughtily answered: "No, their Majesties ordered me to submit to whatever Bobadilla might command; by their authority I was put in chains, and by their authority alone shall they be removed." Fernando tells us that his father was in the habit of keeping the manacles in his cabinet, and that he requested that they might be buried with him.

After a prosperous voyage, the ship reached the port of Cadiz in November, 1500.

CHAPTER VI.

THE FOURTH VOYAGE.

THE arrival of Columbus in chains at the port of Cadiz produced a deep sensation. It was but natural that there should be an instantaneous reaction in his favour. Even those who had not hesitated to criticise or even denounce him, were now moved with a deep and natural sympathy at the ignominy that had over-taken him. The reaction took possession of all classes, and the agitation of the community was scarcely less than it had been when, seven years before, with banners flying and music sounding, he had departed from the same port with a fleet of seventeen ships for his second voyage.

The tidings of his imprisonment soon spread abroad. In the luxurious city of Seville there was deep and general indignation. The court was at Granada. Columbus, still ignorant as to how far the course of Bobadilla had received royal authority, ab-stained from writing to the monarchs. While on shipboard, however, he had written an elaborate letter to Donna Juana de la Torres, formerly a nurse of Prince Juan, and still a great favourite of the queen. The letter was doubtless written in the supposition

that it would reach the court without delay; and with
the permission of the master of the ship, it was despatched by the hand of Antonio de Torres, a friend
of Columbus and a brother of Juana.   Las Casas
tells us that it was by this letter that Ferdinand and
Isabella first learned of the indignities that had been
heaped upon the Admiral.   Other tidings, however,
soon followed.   A friendly letter from Vallejo confirmed in all essential points the narrative of Columbus.   A despatch was also received from the alcalde
to whose hands Columbus had been consigned to
await the pleasure of the sovereigns.

Ferdinand and Isabella acted without hesitation.
Las Casas tells us that the queen was deeply agitated
by the letter of Columbus.   Even the more prudent
Ferdinand did not deem it necessary to wait for the
despatches from Bobadilla.   They declared at once
that the commissioner had exceeded his instructions,
and ordered that Columbus should not only be set
free, but should be treated with every consideration.
They invited him to court, and ordered a credit of
two thousand ducats (a sum equal to more than ten
thousand dollars at the present day) to defray his
expenses.

Columbus reached the court at Granada on the
17th of December.   His hearing before the king and
queen is said not to have been that of a man who had
been disgraced and humiliated, but rather that of one
whose proud spirit was meeting undeserved reproach
with a lofty scorn.   He was richly dressed, and attended with a retinue becoming his high office.   The

king and queen received him with unqualified distinction, and encouraged him with gracious expressions of favour. At length, regaining his self-possession, Columbus delivered an earnest vindication of his course. He explained what he had done, declaring that if at any time he had erred, it had been through inexperience in government, and the extraordinary difficulties under which he had laboured.

Isabella replied in a speech that did great credit to her discretion as well as her sympathy. She declared that while she fully appreciated the magnitude of his services and the rancour of his enemies, she feared that he had given cause for complaint. Charlevoix has reported what purports to be the speech of the queen.

"Common report," she said, "accuses you of acting with a degree of severity quite unsuitable for an infant colony, and likely to excite rebellion there. But the matter as to which I find it hardest to give you my pardon is your conduct in reducing to slavery a number of Indians who had done nothing to deserve such a fate. This was contrary to my express orders. As your ill fortune willed it, just at the time when I heard of this breach of my instructions, everybody was complaining of you, and no one spoke a word in your favour. And I felt obliged to send to the Indies a commissioner to investigate matters and give me a true report, and, if necessary, to put limits to the authority which you were accused of overstepping. If you were found guilty of the charges, he was to relieve you of the government and to send you to Spain to give an account of your stewardship. This was the extent of his commission. I find that I have made a bad choice in my agent, and I shall take care to make an example of Bobadilla which will serve as a warning to others not to exceed their powers. I cannot, however, promise to reinstate you at once in your government. People are too much inflamed against you, and must have time to cool. As to your rank of Admiral, I never intended to deprive you of it. But you must abide your time and trust in me."

The course pursued by the monarchs was not altogether above reproach; for in their haste to make amends to Columbus, they were not unwilling to throw an unjust imputation upon Bobadilla. Whatever had been the intention of the monarchs, it is now plain that the commissioner had not exceeded his authority in making the arrest; and that the monarchs should be willing to dismiss their agent without waiting even to receive his report, is evidence that they had either forgotten the nature of their instructions, or that they were now carried away by the representations of the Admiral or the clamours of the populace.

The Admiral, however, had but little reason to be satisfied. He cared not so much for the removal of Bobadilla as for his own reinstatement. This he deemed necessary to a complete vindication; but in this he was doomed to disappointment. There is no evidence that Ferdinand ever looked with favour on the restoration of Columbus to his command.

The misfortune that had befallen the Admiral was of a nature to awaken sympathy in every generous mind. Even down to the present day this feeling is so wide spread that it is difficult to secure a judicious discrimination between the fact of his removal and the manner in which the removal was accomplished. But these two phases of the subject are entirely distinct, and ought to be independently considered. The manner of the removal can have no justification. This was admitted by the monarchs, who in order to shield themselves from obloquy were not unwilling to bring an unjust charge against the commissioner. It is now plain that the fault of Bobadilla was not in exceeding his authority, but in the unwise and immoderate use of the discretion that had been placed in his hands. It is by no means certain that a careful investigation of affairs in the island, followed by a judicious and moderate report, would not have resulted in a removal of the Admiral from his command ; for it is quite possible that even if Columbus was not deserving of censure, the relations of the different interests were in such turmoil that a governor who had had no connection with affairs thus far, would be more successful in subduing anarchy and in bringing order out of chaos.

But whether such a result would have ensued, can never be more than a matter of mere conjecture. It is certain that the difficulties of the situation had not been successfully overcome by Columbus or by either of his brothers. It is incontestable that even as late as the arrival of Bobadilla, affairs on the island were in great confusion, and that the rebellion had been subdued only by the granting of terms that were not very creditable either to Columbus or to Spanish civilization.

There is nothing remaining that throws more light on the condition of affairs in Hispaniola at the time of which we are speaking, than the letter of Columbus to the old nurse of Don Juan. Any one who reads it thoughtfully must receive a number of very heterogeneous impressions. With a little more than usual intensity, it breathes a loyal and pietistic spirit. It conveys a very delicate, but at the same time a very just, reproach to the monarchs for bestowing on Bobadilla the authority which he received. Nothing could have been more justly or felicitously expressed than the sentence in which he declared: "I have been wounded extremely by the thought that a man should have been sent out to make inquiry into my conduct who knew that if he sent home a very aggravated account of the result of his investigation, he would remain at the head of the government." He showed, moreover, the unpardonable precipitancy with which Bobadilla had acted, in making his arrests right and left before he had had time to conduct any proper investigations.

But after all these mitigations are admitted, and after Columbus has received every credit that can be accorded him, there still remains the fact that the island had been in turmoil almost from the first; that the Indians, who, according to the testimony of Columbus himself, had been at the first everywhere friendly and peaceable, had now become universally hostile; that even if these disorders had largely occurred in the absence of the Admiral, it was nevertheless true that they had all occurred under officers appointed by Columbus himself; that even if, as he said, vast numbers of men had gone to the Indies "who did not deserve water from God or man," still, all the men that had gone had been accepted for the purpose by the Admiral himself; that if he complained that the Spanish settlers "would give as much for a woman as for a farm," and that "this sort of trading is very common," still this iniquity was all under an administration of which he himself was the head, and directly under subordinates whom he himself had appointed to command and, most important of all, under a system which he himself had recommended, and for which he alone was responsible. It may well be asserted that the comprehensive nature of his own commission, and the fact that his appointments had not been interfered with, estopped him from asserting that all responsibility for failure was to be charged to the wickedness and the weakness of his subordinates. Had Columbus been completely adequate to the situation, he would have bound his subordinates to him in unquestioning loyalty. The truth is, however, that from first to last, with the exception of his brothers, those who were nearest him in command sooner or later became his enemies, — and generally the enmity was not long delayed.

But there were other considerations that led Ferdinand to hesitate. The colony had not been prosperous from any point of view. It had been a continuous and unlessening source of expense, and had brought as yet very small returns. The hopes that the early reports of Columbus had aroused had ended in disappointment. The Admiral had confidently expected to come upon all the wealth of the Great Khan and of Cathay. Even the gold mines of Ophir, which he believed he had at length discovered, brought no returns.

In the mean time, however, the court was besieged with the importunities of enterprising navigators who desired permission to make explorations without governmental support. The only favour they asked was the privilege of sailing and of bringing back to the royal treasury the due quota of their gains. They promised to plant the Spanish standard in all the lands of the west, and thus, without depleting the treasury, maintain and even advance the glories of the Spanish discoveries.

To such importunities the Government began to yield as early as 1495. The privileges that were granted were in obvious violation of the exclusive rights bestowed upon Columbus before the first voyage. But it was not easy to observe the letter of that contract. The lands discovered were so much vaster in extent than even Columbus had anticipated that it would be unreasonable to expect a comprehensive observance of the monopoly granted. Though the Admiral made repeated and not unreasonable complaints of the privileges bestowed upon others in violation of his charter, yet the custom of granting such privileges was never completely discontinued. Nor would it have been reasonable to suppose that a monopoly of navigation and government in the western world could forever remain exclusively in the sacred possession of a single family. It was simply a question as to when that monopoly should cease. That there was no purpose to do injustice, was shown in the requirement that the interests of Columbus in the products of the island should be respected to the letter by Bobadilla and his successors.

During the eight years that had now elapsed since the first voyage of the Admiral, a considerable number of navigators had already immortalized themselves by important discoveries and explorations. The Cabots, going out from Bristol, where they had doubtless learned of the projects and the success of Columbus, sailed westward by a more northerly route, and after reaching the continent a year before South America was touched by the Spanish navigator, explored the coast as far as from Newfoundland to Florida. As early as 1487, after seventy years of slow advances down the six thousand miles of western African coast, the Portuguese, under Bartholomew Diaz, as we have already noted, had reached the Cape of Good Hope; and ten years later, just as Columbus was preparing for his third voyage, Vasca da Gama doubled the Cape, and in the following spring cast anchor in the bay at Calicut. In the spring of 1499 Pedro Alonzo Nino, who had accompanied Columbus as a pilot in the voyage to Cuba and Paria, obtained a license, and not only explored the coast of Central America for several hundred miles, but traded his European goods to such advantage as to enable him to return after one of the most extensive and lucrative voyages yet accomplished. In the same year, Vincente Yanez Pinzon, who had

commanded one of the ships in the first expedition of
Columbus, pushed boldly to the southwest, and, crossing the equator, came finally to the great headland
which is now known as Cape St. Augustine, and for
their Catholic Majesties not only took possession of
the territories called the Brazils, but discovered what
was afterwards appropriately named the River of the
Amazons. In the year 1500 Diego Lepe, fired with
the zeal for discovery that had set the port of Palos
aglow, went still farther to the south, and, turning Cape
St. Augustine, ascertained that either the mainland or
an enormous island ran far away to the southwest.

Most important and significant of all, the fleet which,
in the year 1500, was sent out from Portugal under
Pedro Cabral, for the Cape of Good Hope, in striving,
according to the advice of Da Gama, to avoid the dangers of the coast islands, drifted so far west that when
it was caught in a violent easterly storm, it was driven
upon the coast of Brazil, and thus proved that even if
Columbus had not lived and sailed, America would
have been made known to Europe in the very first
year of the sixteenth century.

Thus it was that, not to speak in detail of the explorations of navigators of lesser note, the English
explorers in the north, and the Spanish and Portuguese in the south, had, before the end of the year
1500, given to Europe a definite, though an incorrect,
conception of the magnitude of the new world. There
is no evidence that as yet anybody had supposed the
newly discovered lands to be any other than the eastern borders of Asia and Africa. But it must have been

evident enough to many others, as well as to King
Ferdinand, that these new possessions were too vast
and too important to be intrusted to the governorship
of any one man. They appealed alike to ambition,
to avarice, and to jealousy.

The policy adopted was one of delay. Columbus
was naturally impatient to return to the office of
which he had been deprived. The court, however,
while treating him with every external consideration,
would not bring itself to give an affirmative answer.
Another course was finally adopted. It was agreed
that Bobadilla should be removed, that another governor, who had had no part in the administrative
quarrels, should be appointed for a term of two years,
and that Columbus should be intrusted with a new
exploring expedition.

The person chosen to supersede Bobadilla was
Nicholas de Ovando, a commander of the Order of
Alcantara. The picture given of him by Las Casas is
one that might well conciliate the prepossessions of the
reader. According to this high authority, he was gracious in manner, fluent in speech, had great veneration
for justice, was an enemy to avarice, and had such an
aversion to ostentation that when he arose to be grand
commander, he would never allow himself to be addressed by the title attaching to his office. Yet he
was a man of ardent temper, and so, in the opinion of
Las Casas, was incapable of governing the Indians,
upon whom he inflicted incalculable injury.

Before Ovando was ready to sail, there was considerable delay. It had been decided to give him com-

mand, not only of Hispaniola, but also of the other islands and of the mainland. The fleet was to be the largest yet sent to the western world. When at length it was ready, it mustered thirty sail, and had on board about twenty-five hundred souls.

That the new governor might appear with becoming dignity, he was allowed an unusual amount of ostentation. A sumptuous attire of silk brocades and precious stones was prescribed, and he was permitted a body-guard of seventy-two yeomen.

Las Casas accompanied this expedition, and consequently we have the great advantage of his own personal observations. He tells us that a great crowd of adventurers thronged the fleet, — "eager speculators, credulous dreamers, and broken-down gentlemen of desperate fortunes, — all expecting to enrich themselves with little effort." But it is evident also that there was another class on which greater hopes might reasonably be placed. In the original accounts, significant attention is called to the fact that among those who formed the expedition there were seventy-three married men with their families, all of respectable character. Among those enumerated we notice, not only a chief-justice to replace Roldan, but a physician, a surgeon, and an apothecary, — in short, persons of all ranks that seemed to be necessary for the supply and the development of the island.

That the sovereigns were not unmindful of the rights of Columbus, was evinced by the provisions made for the protection of his interests. Ovando was ordered to examine into all the accounts, for the

purpose of ascertaining the amount of the damages
Columbus had suffered. All the property belonging
to the Admiral that had been confiscated by Bobadilla was to be restored, and the same care was to
be taken of the interests of the Admiral's brothers.
Not only were the arrears of the revenues to be paid,
but they were also to be secured for the future. To
this end Columbus was permitted to have an agent
present at the smelting and the working of the gold,
in order that his own rights might be duly protected.

But notwithstanding these evidences of royal favour,
the Admiral was much depressed in spirit. In the
course of the long months during which he was condemned to wait for the final action of the sovereigns,
he had much time for reflection ; and it is not singular that his thoughts turned to his long-neglected
scheme for the rescue of the Holy Sepulchre. From
the years of his early manhood, the desirability of
such an act had held possession of his soul. It
was characteristic of his immoderate ardour that he
even recorded a vow that within seven years from
the time of the discovery he would furnish fifty thousand foot soldiers and four thousand horse for the
accomplishment of this purpose. The time had
elapsed, and the vow remained unfulfilled. It had
not, however, passed out of his remembrance ; and he
now appealed to the monarchs to take the matter up
as a national enterprise. The war with Granada
had come to a victorious end ; the Duke of Medina
Sidonia had given new lustre to the Spanish name in
Italy ; the Spanish armies were now at leisure ; Ferdi-

nand and Isabella were firm supporters of the Church :
and what could be more appropriate than that they
should now prove their superior devotion and power
by the vigorous presecution of an enterprise that had
baffled the efforts of united Christendom for more
than two centuries? The visionary element in the
mind of Columbus was never more plainly revealed.

These dreamy speculations and importunities, however, were only temporary in their nature. The mind
of the explorer soon reverted to more practical affairs.
It was spurred on in this direction and in that by the
successes of Portuguese explorers in the East. Vasco
da Gama had shown that navigation beyond the Cape
of Good Hope was practicable, and Pedro Cabral
had not only gone as far as the marts of Hindostan,
but had returned with ships laden with precious commodities of infinite variety. The discoveries in the
West had thus far brought no return ; and yet, according to every theory that Columbus had entertained, the islands he had discovered were only the
border-land — only the fringe, so to speak — of that
vast Eastern region that was flaming with Oriental
gold. There must be a passage from the west that
opened into the Indian Sea. The coast of Paria
stretched on toward the west, the southern coast of
Cuba extended in the same direction, and the currents of the Caribbean Sea seemed to indicate that
at some point still farther west there was a strait that
connected the waters of the Atlantic and the Indian
Ocean. To discover such a passage was an ambition
worthy even of the lofty spirits of Columbus. He

believed that somewhere west or southwest of the
lands he had discovered such a strait would be found;
and it was to find such a passage that he resolved
to undertake a fourth voyage.

Columbus appears to have remained at Granada
with the court from December of 1499 until late in
the year 1501. He then repaired to Seville, where
he was able within a few months to fit out an exploring squadron of four ships. The insignificant size of
vessels of those days may be inferred from the fact
that, according to Fernando, the largest of the ships
was of seventy tons' burden, and the smallest of fifty.
The crew consisted of one hundred and fifty men and
boys, among whom were the Admiral's brother, Don
Bartholomew, and his son Fernando, the historian.

There were long and unaccountable delays, and
the fleet did not sail from Cadiz before the 9th of
May, 1502. Stopping for further supplies at St.
Catherine's and Arzilla, as well as at the Grand
Canary and Martinique, it was not until the 25th
that the westward voyage for the Indies was fairly
begun. The first design was to go directly to the
coast of Paria; but although the voyage was an un-
usually smooth one, Columbus, declaring one of the
vessels to be unseaworthy, or at least to be in great
need of repairs, decided to make for St. Domingo in
order to effect an exchange of vessels. This port
was safely reached before the end of June; but the
object of his coming was destined to be speedily
frustrated.

To avoid the consequences of a surprise, Columbus

had taken the precaution to send one of his captains
with despatches to inform Ovando of his approach
and the nature of his errand. Besides referring to
the condition of one of the ships, he begged the
privilege of temporary shelter for his fleet. Columbus
himself, in his letter, says nothing of any motive, excepting his desire to purchase a vessel to take the
place of the one that had become disabled ; but Fernando attributes to him the additional purpose of
securing shelter from a violent storm which he saw
to be impending. According to his son's doubtful
authority, the Admiral even ventured to advise that
the departure of the fleet about to sail for Spain, with
the treasures that Bobadilla had collected, should be
delayed until the coming storm was past. Columbus
himself, however, never made any such claim. But
no part of the message was of any avail. It was
evident that the new commander, Ovando, who had
now been several months in power, was not free
from ill-will toward the Admiral. Las Casas is of
the opinion that he had received secret instructions
from the sovereigns not to admit the Admiral to the
island. It seems certain that at that time San Domingo abounded with enemies of Columbus, and
the decision may have been reached simply by considerations of prudence. The hospitality of the harbour was refused, and the outgoing fleet of eighteen
sail was not detained.

Denied the privilege of the harbour, Columbus drew
his little fleet up under the shelter of the island. On
the last day of June a terrible hurricane broke upon

them. The vessels were torn from their moorings, and driven apart into the wide sea. Each of the ships lost sight of the others, and each supposed that all the others were lost. The fury of the winds and waves continued throughout many days and nights; and such was the raging tumult of the elements that it seemed impossible for a single vessel to escape. By what was considered a miraculous interposition of Providence, however, all the ships of Columbus outrode the storm. The fact that the "unseaworthy" vessel survived with the others, gives colour to the suspicion that the claim of unseaworthiness was only a pretence for the purpose of getting access to the port. The vessel which the Admiral commanded was driven as far as Jamaica; and if we may believe the sweeping and unqualified language of the Admiral, "during sixty days there was no cessation of the tempest, which was one continuation of rain, thunder, and lightning." In this same connection Columbus writes to the sovereigns: "Eighty-eight days did this fearful tempest continue, during which I was at sea, and saw neither sun nor stars. My ships lay exposed, with sails torn; and anchors, cables, rigging, boats, and a great quantity of provisions were lost. My people were very weak and humbled in spirit, many of them promising to lead a religious life, and all making vows and promising to perform pilgrimages, while some of them would frequently go to their messmates to make confession. Other tempests have been experienced, but never of so long a duration or so fearful as this."

But if the Admiral was finally successful in bringing the shattered remains of his fleet together, it was not until the 12th of September that they reached the place of safety and promise to which the commander gave the name Gracios à Dios. It was far otherwise with the larger squadron. The commander, after refusing to heed the predictions of the Admiral, had just set out for Spain. On board were Bobadilla and Roldan, as well as the others that had taken a prominent part in accusing Columbus, and securing his arrest and imprisonment. The vessels were also laden with so much gold and other articles of value as a relentless avarice and cruelty could bring together to justify the administration. The details of the disaster have not been preserved. All that we know is that of the eighteen vessels only four escaped complete destruction. Every important personage on board the fleet was lost. Of the four less unfortunate ships, three were in such a shattered condition that they were obliged to return to San Domingo, while only one, "The Needle," was able to make its way to Spain. To the unquestioning religious faith of the time, the proof of providential direction was made complete by the singular fact that the gold on board "The Needle," the poorest vessel of the fleet, was the portion that belonged to Columbus. Las Casas regards the event as a signal example of those awful judgments with which Providence sometimes overwhelms those who have incurred divine displeasure.

For a knowledge of the explorations of Columbus during the fourth voyage we are indebted to a very elaborate letter of the Admiral himself, and to the accounts by Fernando, Las Casas, and Porras, all of whom were, at the time, either with the Admiral or at San Domingo. The accounts do not agree in all particulars, but essentially they are not unlike. As to the general course of the expedition, and the reasons for the course taken, there is substantial agreement.

At the end of the succession of storms in the autumn of 1502 Columbus found himself among the islands south of Cuba. The way was now open for the prosecution of the design which had led to the organization of the expedition. He was in search of an open passage. His idea, of course, could not have been very clearly defined ; for he still believed that the islands he had already visited were only the remote edge of the Asiatic continent. As yet he had no reason for definite belief as to whether Cuba was an island or was a part of the mainland ; though, as we have already seen, he had once required his crew to swear on their return that it was the mainland, under penalty of having their tongues wrenched out in case of disobedience. As his purpose now was avowedly that of an explorer pure and simple, it would seem that three ways were clearly open to him. He had already in his second voyage made himself sufficiently familiar with eastern Cuba to know that whether an island or a part of the mainland, it was a vast projection into the east ; and he must have inferred that its relations with the regions beyond could most easily and naturally be ascertained by sailing in a westerly direction, either along the northern or along the southern coast. The other course open to him was a bold push for new regions by sailing into the open sea to the southwest. The obvious disadvantage of this course was the fact that whatever might be discovered, the relations of the new regions to those already explored would still be involved in mystery. Whether Cuba were an island or a part of the continent, could not in this way be determined. In the way of promised advantages, moreover, this direction would seem to have held out no greater inducements than either of the others. If he had sailed along the northern coast of Cuba, he would have determined the fact of its insularity, and then would have been free to explore farther for the mainland. But the more promising course was on the other side of the island; for in this way the source of the currents, on which the navigator placed so much reliance, could have been traced, — or at least it could have been determined whether the phenomenal flow of waters originated, as Columbus supposed, in an open strait. The least promising course of all was the abandonment of Cuba and the striking out of an independent course to the southwest; for when land should be reached, there could be no determination whether the new coast had any connection with the land already discovered, and it would still be undetermined whether the strait for which he was searching, if it existed at all, lay to the east or to the west of the new landfall. But this least promising course was the one Columbus determined to take. It was a great blunder, for which no good reason has ever been given.

Sailing in a southwesterly direction, the storms still continuing, he at length approached the mainland at a small island which he called the Isle of Pines. He then turned to the east, and in a few days reached the coast of Honduras. After waiting for a short time to trade with the natives, he kept on his way in the same general direction, in the face of a stormy current and violent winds. It was not until the 14th of September that they rounded the cape which in thankfulness to God he named Cape Gracios à Dios. At this point the current divided, a part flowing west, and a part south. Taking advantage of the latter, they proceeded down the Mosquito coast without difficulty. On the 25th of September they came to an inviting spot which he called the "Garden." The natives seemed more intelligent than any Columbus had yet seen. In order that he might have a supply of interpreters, the Admiral seized seven of them, two of whom he retained by force even when, October 5, he sailed away. This forcible detention was greatly resented by the tribe, but the prayers of the emissaries sent for their release had no effect.

Pushing still farther south and east, the Spaniards came in about ten days to Caribaro Bay. The natives, who wore gold plates as ornaments, were defiant, and expressed their unwelcoming mood by blasts upon conch-shells and the brandishing of spears. The Spanish lombards, however, soon brought them to a more submissive spirit. A little farther along, the vessels came to Varagua, a territory lying just west of the Isthmus of Darien. Here the Admiral heard glowing accounts of gold not far away. His inter-

preters told him that ten days inland the natives rev-
elled in the precious metals and all other valuable
commodities. Had he listened and obeyed, he would
have discovered the Pacific. But, for once, he turned
a deaf ear to the allurement, and so lost his opportunity. That the natives hinted at the great waters
beyond the isthmus, is plain from the words of Columbus. He says: "They say that the sea surrounds
Cuguare, and that ten days' journey from thence is
the river Ganges."

His farther voyage south brought no important results. The ships were worm-eaten, and the crew
were clamorous for the gold of Varagua. On the 5th
of December Columbus decided reluctantly to retrace
his course. By one of those singular adversities of
fortune, the winds which had hitherto blown strongly
from the east now veered and blew as strongly from
the west. Gale after gale followed. Columbus called
it the "Coast of Contrasts." The situation of the
navigators became all the more desperate through the
horrors of impending famine. Worms had made their
bread revolting, and the crew were driven to catch
sharks for food.

For weeks the violence of the storms continued.
In attempting to make their way back, a full month
was taken up by the Spaniards in passing a hundred
miles. The whole winter was consumed without
important results. At Varagua earnest hopes were
entertained that the long-sought, but ever-elusive
gold-fields were at length to be found. Columbus
says that he saw more indications of gold in two
days than he had seen in Hispaniola in four years;

he therefore decided upon a settlement, and began to build houses. Eighty members of the crew were to be left to establish a permanent footing.

But misfortune succeeded misfortune. The natives began to organize for the purpose of making such a settlement impossible. In one of their conflicts the cacique, known as the Quibian, was taken prisoner by the Adelantado. He was intrusted to the care of a Spanish officer, who imprudently yielded to the chief's persuasions to remove his shackles. The consequence was that in an unguarded moment the cacique sprang over the side of the boat and dived to the bottom. The night was dark, and as he came to the surface he was not detected. Columbus believed him drowned; but it soon appeared that he had reached the shore and organized so formidable an opposition to the settlement as to place the colony in extreme peril.

Provisions and ammunition now began to run short. The Admiral was tortured with gout, and this was followed by a fever. While affairs were in this condition a portion of the prisoners threw open a hatchway, and, thrusting the guards aside, plunged into the sea and escaped. Those who had failed to get away were thrust back into the hold; but in the morning it was found that they had all committed suicide by hanging. The resolute spirit thus shown was a sad foreboding of disaster. The sea was so rough that for days there could be no communication between the Admiral on ship and the Adelantado on shore. When at length a brave swimmer succeeded in reaching the land, he found a portion of Bartholomew's force in revolt. The mutineers formed a plan to desert the commander and effect an escape to the ships. There was nothing to do but to rescue the colony, if possible, and abandon the coast.

When affairs appeared to be in a most hopeless condition, the tempest abated, and fair weather came on. One of the caravels, however, had been stranded and wrecked. In order to bring off the stores and the colony, a raft was constructed, and after long effort the survivors were rescued and taken aboard the remaining vessels. One of these, however, proved to be so much worm-eaten and otherwise disabled that it had to be abandoned. Taking the scanty stores into the two remaining caravels, the adventurers now turned their prows toward Hispaniola.

The course of the vessels, however, in order to meet the strong westerly currents, was eastward. The crew were thrown into consternation by the thought that the Admiral, notwithstanding the unseaworthy condition of the ships, was making for Spain. But Columbus had no such purpose. His design was to zigzag his course in such a manner that none of the crew could find the way back to the gold coast. He says that he remembered how a former crew had returned to the pearl-fisheries of Paria; and he now wrote: "None of them can explain whither I went, nor whence I came. They do not know the way to return thither.".

Having accomplished his bewildering purpose, the Admiral now turned to the northwest. Falling into the currents, the vessels floated beyond Hispaniola; and on the 30th of May they found themselves in the group of islands which Columbus had already called

"The Gardens." That his old delusion was still kept up, is evident from his declaration that he "had come to Mango, which is near Cathay."

Here again a succession of storms came on and threatened to shatter the crazy hulks to pieces. Columbus tried to find shelter in the lee of one of the islands; but he lost all his anchors save one, and the crews were able to keep the ships afloat only by "three pumps, and the use of their pots and kettles." Evidently this condition of affairs could not long continue. On the 23d of June he reached Jamaica, and a little later he saw no other course than to run both of his ships aground. The first he ran ashore on the 23d of July; and on the 12th of August he brought the other alongside, and managed to lash them together. The tide soon filled them with water. He built cabins on the forecastles, in which the crew could live until they could find relief.

The navigators' scanty supply of food was ruined, and their first thought, therefore, was to barter for supplies with the natives. Fortunately, they were successful. Diego Mendez, the commander of one of the vessels, took the matter in hand, and making the circuit of the island in company with three other Spaniards, bargained advantageously with several of the caciques.

The next thought of the Admiral was to send to Ovando for a rescuing vessel. He proposed to Mendez that he should go in an open boat, as the only possible means of establishing a connection with San Domingo. Mendez offered to go in case no one else would volunteer. The others all held back. He then fitted up a row-boat, and taking one other Spaniard and six natives as oarsmen, committed himself to a voyage of nearly two hundred miles in those tempestuous waters.

To Mendez, Columbus committed a long letter addressed to the monarchs of Spain, — the very letter, no doubt, to which we are indebted for much of our knowledge of this disastrous voyage. It bears date July 7, 1503, and may well be regarded as the unmistakable evidence of a distracted, if not of an unbalanced, mind.

Though the writer had much to say of the voyage, the most prominent characteristic of the writing was its rambling and incoherent references to the troubles of his earlier years. It was a veritable appeal *ad misericordiam*, and was full of inaccuracies, not to say positive misstatements. He says, —

"I was twenty-eight years old when I came into your Highnessès' services, and now I have not a hair upon me that is not gray, my body is infirm, and all that was left to me, as well as to my brother, has been taken away and sold, even to the frock that I wore, to my great dishonour. Solitary in my trouble, sick, and in daily expectation of death, I am surrounded by millions of hostile savages full of cruelty. Weep for me whoever has charity, truth, and justice."

Surely this is not the outpouring of a great soul. On the contrary, it is simply pitiful; for it is impossible to forget that in earlier years he had described these "millions of hostile savages" as the embodiment of hospitable kindness. It was not until the innocent natives had learned by bitter experience that there was no device of avarice or cruelty or licentiousness of which they were not made the victims that their unsuspecting hospitality was turned into a prudent hostility. If Columbus was only twenty-eight when he entered the service of the Spanish monarchs, he must have been born in 1456; he must have been only eighteen when he had the correspondence with Toscanelli; and at the time of his writing, he must have been only forty-seven. Recurring to geographical affairs, he writes: "The world is but small; out of seven divisions of it, the dry part occupies six, and the seventh is entirely covered with water. I say that the world is not so large as vulgar opinion makes it." Referring to his search for gold, he exclaims: "Gold is the most precious of all commodities; gold constitutes treasure; and he who possesses it has all the needs of this world, as also the means of rescuing souls from Purgatory and introducing them to the enjoyments of Paradise."

After the departure of Mendez the long months of autumn and winter wore on. Columbus during much of the time was confined to his bed by illness. Discontents, and finally insubordination, became rife. The malcontents put themselves under the leadership of Francisco de Porras, a daring navigator, who at one time had commanded one of the vessels. On the 2d of January, 1504, Porras appeared in the cabin of the sick Admiral. An unfortunate altercation ensued, which resulted in dividing the little band into

two hostile camps.   The outcome was that Porras and
forty-one others threw themselves into active rebellion.
They took forcible possession of ten canoes, and committed themselves to the sea with the mad purpose of
going to San Domingo.   A short experience, however,
was enough to drive them back, and they now devoted
themselves actively to getting supplies from the natives
of Jamaica.   This of course interfered greatly with
the comforts of Columbus and his little band.   Indeed
it might have proved fatal but for one of those ingenious expedients of which the mind of the Admiral
was so prolific.

An eclipse of the moon was to take place on the
night of February 29, 1504.   Columbus caused it
to be widely circulated among the natives that the
God of the Spaniards was greatly displeased with
their lack of loyalty, and was about to manifest his
displeasure by an obscuration of the moon.   As the
eclipse came on, the words of the Admiral appeared
to be verified.   The natives were convulsed with fear.
He now declared that the divine anger would be ap-
peased if they would show proper contrition and
would furnish the needed supplies.   The caciques
threw themselves at his feet, and promised everything
he might need.   Just before the moon was to emerge
from the shadow, he assured them that the divine
wrath was placated, and that a sign would soon be
manifested.   As the eclipse passed off, the astonish-
ment and satisfaction of the poor wretches were complete.   From that time Columbus had no lack of
sufficient supplies.

The expedition of Mendez was not without the most trying vicissitudes. Almost immediately after starting, the little bark encountered so heavy a sea that it was obliged to turn back. A few days later, however, another boat was ready, and Mendez committed himself a second time to this daring enterprise. Rough weather was encountered, and for a considerable period it seemed that all would be lost. One of the natives died, and his body was cast into the sea. But at length, in four days after leaving the eastern point of Jamaica, the Spaniards reached the port of Novissa, at the western end of Hispaniola. Mendez soon found that Ovando, instead of being at San Domingo, was engaged in suppressing a revolt in the western province of Zaroyna. Though Ovando was not so ungracious as to meet the question with a point-blank refusal, he showed no disposition to render prompt assistance. Thus it was that, in spite of all the urgency of Mendez, month after month passed away without action. It was only after there had come to be considerable popular clamour in favour of Columbus that Ovando saw the expediency of sending the necessary succour. It is more than probable that he would have been relieved to find that the rescuing ship had arrived too late. It was not until the 25th of June, 1504, that the Admiral and his little crew of wretched followers were gladdened by the sight of approaching relief. It is easy to understand how Columbus, a little later, could say that in no part of his life did he ever experience so joyful a day; for he had never hoped to leave the place

alive.   More than a year had passed in the torment-
ing experiences that followed the shipwreck on the
northern coast of Jamaica.

Ovando extended to Columbus a gracious show of
hospitality by making him a guest in his own household.   But there was no real cordiality.   It was not
long, indeed, before an active dispute arose over
an important question of jurisdiction.   Ovando demanded the surrender of Porras, that he might be
duly punished for his insurrection.   Columbus held
that however complete the jurisdiction of the governor
might be over the island of Hispaniola, it did not extend to the crew of the Admiral.   Ovando, though
he did not formally yield the point, thought it not
prudent to press the claim.   There were also important differences in regard to the pecuniary rights
of Columbus, whose agent had already become
involved in serious difficulties.   From all these
untoward circumstances it became apparent that
the stay of Columbus could not be advantageously
prolonged.   Accordingly, with such money as he
could collect, he fitted out two vessels for a homeward voyage.   He had arrived at San Domingo on
the 15th of August.   On the 12th of the following
month the two vessels were ready for sea.   Storm
succeeded storm, however, and the ship of the Admiral had to be sent back for repairs.   After a very
tempestuous voyage, Columbus, with his brother and
son, entered the port of San Lucar on the 7th of
November, 1504.

CHAPTER VII.

LAST DAYS. —— DEATH. —— CHARACTER.

THE career of Columbus was now practically at an end. From the port he went to Seville, where, broken in health as well as in spirit, he was obliged to remain for nearly four months. We find that on the 23d of February, 1505, a royal order was issued to furnish him with a mule, that he might have an easy seat in his journey toward the court at Segovia. He appears in the course of the year to have found his way to Salamanca, and then to have followed the court to Valladolid ; but farther he was not able to go.

During the year and a half that was left to him after his return from the fourth voyage, Columbus exerted himself constantly and in various ways to improve his personal interests. He had much leisure for writing ; and, fortunately, his letters have been preserved and published in the collection of Navarrete. It would perhaps have been better for his fame if they had not survived ; for while the errors and contradictions perplex every thoughtful reader, the spirit breathed throughout is one of petulancy and comprehensive censure. He rehearsed in various forms the story of his early efforts, of his unappreciated labours, of his

services in behalf of the Crown, and of failure to receive the proper recognition and reward. Unfortunately, the death of Queen Isabella occurred only a
few days after his return. This melancholy event not
only withdrew from the service of Columbus the most
important of all patrons, but it so absorbed all the
attention of the court that his claims received no
attention whatever. To his repeated importunities
no answer came for some months. The king had
always been either indifferent or inimical. The statements of Porras had been received, and they had
evidently made an impression unfavourable to Columbus. The inference from the attitude of the court is
inevitable that in the course of the two and a half
years of the Admiral's absence during his fourth voyage
his popularity had so declined that he had almost
ceased to be regarded as a person of importance. It
is certain that the complaints against him had now
made so strong an impression on the king and on
those in authority that there was no disposition to
listen to his importunities.

Still, Columbus continued to write. In one letter
he arraigned the administration of Ovando, charging
it with the same crimes that had so often been alleged
against himself. He declared that the governor was
detested by all; that a suitable person could restore
order in three months; that the abuses should at once
be remedied by the appointment of a judicious successor; that new fortresses should be at once built, —
"all of which," he says, "I can do in his Highness's
service; and any other, not having my personal inter-

est at stake, cannot do it as well." At another time he urges Diego to sue the king for a mandatory letter forcing Ovando to make immediate payment of Columbus's share of the revenues. Concerning Vespucius, who had already returned from his second voyage and written the famous letter of Sept. 4, 1504, he wrote in the following terms: "Within two days I have talked with Americus Vespucius. . . . He has always manifested a disposition to be friendly to me. Fortune has not always favoured him, and in this he is not different from many others. His ventures have not always been as successful as he would wish. He left me full of the kindest purposes toward me, and will do anything for me that is in his power. I did not know what to tell him as to the way in which he could help me, because I knew not why he had been called to court. Find out what he can do, and he will do it; but so manage that he will not be suspected of aiding me." This letter is of most interesting significance, because at the very moment of its date, the letter of Vespucius was making the impression upon Europe which was to eclipse the renown of Columbus and give the name of its author to the western continent. That there was any purpose on the part of Vespucius inimical to the fame of Columbus there is no reason whatever to believe.

The multitudinous letters of Columbus seem to have made no impression. Las Casas says: "The more he petitioned, the more bland the king was in avoiding any conclusion." The same author further declares that Ferdinand "hoped, by exhausting the

patience of the Admiral, to induce him to accept some
estates in Castile in place of his powers in the Indies.
But Columbus rejected all such offers with indignation."

During the later months of 1505, and the early
months of 1506, it was becoming more and more
apparent that preparations for the end must not be
long delayed.   The mind of the Admiral came to be
much occupied with the testamentary disposition of
his rights and titles.   Property in hand he really
seems to have had none ; but he still was not without
hope that in a final settlement his claims in the Indies
would be fully recognized.   Accordingly, in his last
will, which was duly signed and witnessed on the 19th
of May, 1506, he made disposition of his titles and
his rights.   He confirmed his legitimate son, Diego,
his heir ; but in default of heirs of Diego, his rights
were to pass to his illegitimate son, Fernando.   If
in this line there should be a like default, his property was to go to his brother, the Adelantado, and his
male descendants.   If these all should fail, the estate
was to go to the female line in a similar succession.
Two other provisions of the will are worthy of note.
He makes his old scheme of a crusade to recover the
Holy Sepulchre contingent upon the income of the
estate.   He then provides for the maintenance of
Beatrix Enriquez, the mother of Fernando, and says :
" Let this be done for the discharge of my conscience,
for it weighs heavy on my soul, — the reasons for
which I am not here permitted to give."

It was on the 20th of May, 1506, the very next day
after signing the will, that the restless soul of Colum-

bus passed away. His death occurred at Valladolid, in a house that is still shown to interested travellers. It is melancholy to add that the event made no impression either upon the city or upon the nation. We are told, as the result of the most careful search, that the only official document that makes mention of the decease of Columbus is one written by the monarch to Ovando, bearing date of the 2d of June. Neither Bernaldez nor Oviedo designates the day of the month. By the chroniclers of the time, as Harrisse has said, the event seems to have passed " completely unheeded."

Nor is there any certainty as to the place of burial. In the will which Columbus signed just before his death he indicated a desire to have his remains taken to San Domingo. It has generally been supposed, however, that a temporary interment took place in a Franciscan convent at Valladolid. The will of Diego seems to indicate that as early as the year 1513 the coffin containing his remains was conveyed to Seville, where, for nearly or quite thirty years, it rested in the Carthusian convent of Las Cuevas. Royal provisions relating to the removal to San Domingo have been preserved, bearing dates of 1537, 1539, and 1540. From these orders and from the fact that the cathedral at San Domingo was completed in the year 1541, the inference has been drawn that the transfer took place in that year or a little later. There is evidence that the removal had been accomplished before the year 1549.

The controversy that has taken place over the present resting-place of the remains is perhaps enough to justify a somewhat detailed statement of the several points at issue.

Columbus's son Diego and his grandson Luis died respectively in 1526 and 1572. Their remains were also transferred to the cathedral at San Domingo; though at what date there is considerable uncertainty. Some rather obscure records have been discovered in Spain which have been thought to indicate that the removal took place about the beginning of the seventeenth century. Nearly all that we are justified in asserting without qualification is the fact that, from the period of this removal until near the end of the eighteenth century, the cathedral at San Domingo contained the remains of Columbus as well as those of his son and his grandson.

So far as can now be ascertained, there were no inscriptions on the exterior of any of the vaults. The only guide to the site of the exact resting-place of the Admiral was a memorandum in the records of the cathedral to the effect that the body rested in the chancel at the right of the high altar. But as this memorandum bears date of 1676, it could hardly be regarded as anything more than the record of a tradition. During the long period between the early part of the sixteenth century and the end of the eighteenth, the floors of the cathedral were several times repaired; but, so far as is known, the vaults were not disturbed or even discovered.

In the course of the French Revolution the tumult into which San Domingo was thrown resulted in giv-

ing the French so much influence that by the treaty
of Basle, signed on the 22d of July, 1795, Spain
was obliged to cede to France the western portion of
the island. The natural pride of the Spaniards, however, inspired them with a praiseworthy desire to
transfer the remains of the discoverer to Spanish soil.
Accordingly, explorations were made beneath the
floor on the right of the altar of the cathedral. A
vault was found and opened, which contained a small
leaden box and the remains of a human body. Its
situation in the cathedral corresponded with the indications of tradition. The box or casket was in a
very dilapidated condition; but so far as could be
discovered, there was no inscription upon it. No
doubt, however, was entertained in regard to its
genuineness. The contents of the vault were placed
in a gilded sarcophagus, and with great ceremony,
on the 19th of January, 1796, were transported to
Havana. Here they were placed near the high altar
of the cathedral, where, in 1822, the monument was
erected which still adorns the spot and commemorates
the discoveries of the Admiral.

For nearly a century no question was raised as to
the genuineness of the remains thus exhumed and
carried to Havana. But in 1877, in the course of
some changes in the chancel of the cathedral at San
Domingo, two other graves were opened. Each contained a leaden casket. That on the left side of the
altar bore an inscription which, translated into English,
runs : "To the Admiral Don Luis Columbus, duke of
Jamaica, marquis of Veragua." The inscriptions on

the casket which was discovered on the right of the altar were of far more interest and importance.

But before indicating in detail the significance of this discovery, let us take note of the relative position of the vaults. The one containing the casket with the inscription of Luis upon it, was at the extreme left of the chancel and against the wall; while that containing the one which now appeared to hold the remains of the discoverer was next the wall on the opposite side. Adjoining this newly opened vault, and between it and the altar, was the narrower vault, the contents of which had been taken to Havana in 1796. It is natural to infer that the vault situated next the cathedral wall was the first one constructed, and that the smaller and inner vault was added at a later day.

On the newly discovered casket were three inscriptions rudely cut. On the exterior were the three letters "C. C. A.," — probably signifying "Cristoval Colon, Almirante." On the outside of the cover were the abbreviations, " D. de la A. Pre. Ate.," which have been interpreted as standing for " Descubridor de la America, Primero Almirante, — "The Discoverer of America, the first Admiral." On the inside of the cover, in Gothic letters, was an abbreviated inscription which is commonly translated as "The celebrated and extraordinary man, Don Christopher Columbus."

It is to be noted also that there was lying upon the bottom of the casket a small silver plate about three inches in length by one and a third in breadth. Near the ends of this plate were two small holes corresponding with two holes in the posterior wall of the casket. With the plate were also two screws that corresponded in size with the holes in the box and the plate. Very curiously, the plate was found to have an inscription on either side. One of these was simply "Cristoval Colon," while the other, in somewhat abbreviated form, was "Ultima parte de los restos del primero Almirante Cristoval Colon, Descubridor," — "The last remains of the first Admiral, Christopher Columbus, the Discoverer." The significance of these two inscriptions, as it must have been understood that one of them would be concealed by resting against the wall of the box, has been the subject of many conjectures. But the most rational explanation is the supposition that when the engraver had incised the name "Cristoval Colon" on one side, it was found unsatisfactory, from its brevity, and accordingly the more elaborate inscription was placed on the other side. With the contents of this leaden box there was also found a corroded musket-ball. This bullet is supposed to have been in the body of Columbus at the time of his burial. We have no account of his having been wounded while he was in Portugal or Spain, or in the course of any of his voyages; but in his letter to the king written from Jamaica while on his fourth voyage, he says that his wound "had broken out afresh." This expression has led Cronau to conjecture that in some of his earlier maritime experiences, the Admiral had received a bullet which he carried in his body to the end of his life.

The discovery of this casket very naturally awakened the greatest interest in San Domingo, and indeed wherever the story of Columbus was known. The bishop of the cathedral, recognizing the importance of the event, invited to a formal inspection of the remains, not only the representatives of the civil government, but also all the foreign consuls that were present in San Domingo. These united in the belief that the bones of the Admiral were still in the cathedral, and that the remains which had been carried to Havana in 1796 were those of his son Diego. Having arrived at this conclusion, the authorities enclosed the casket, with its contents, in a glass case, and locked it with three keys, two of which were to be guarded by members of the Government, and one by the bishop. They then bound the glass case with ribbons, which were carefully sealed, not only with the seals of the cathedral and of the Government, but also with those of all the foreign consuls then at San Domingo. Finally, they placed the sarcophagus containing the box and the remains in a side chapel of the cathedral.

So full an account of this interesting discovery would hardly have been appropriate, but for the controversy which immediately ensued. The Spanish authorities in the mother-country and in Cuba were very naturally reluctant to believe, except upon the most conclusive evidence, that a mistake had been made in 1796. The cry of fraud was soon raised. The inscriptions, a rough fac-simile of which had been made and published by the bishop, were declared to be the work of a modern forger. Pamphlet after pamphlet was issued from the press, until there came to be a voluminous literature on the subject.

Against the genuineness of the inscriptions there were only two arguments of any considerable weight. The first was in the assertion that the inscriptions were of too modern and crude a nature to have been placed upon the casket in the sixteenth century by those having in charge the moving of the remains. The other was the presence of the abbreviation which was supposed to stand for America. It was confidently alleged that the Spaniards had refused to adopt the name America until after the time of the removal. In both of these objections there seemed to be considerable force. But they cannot be regarded as conclusive; for in the first place a more careful copying of the inscriptions has revealed the fact that they are not so dissimilar to the prevailing methods of the sixteenth century as was at first supposed; and in answer to the second objection, it is to be said that Waldseemüller's book suggesting the name America was published in April of 1507, and that as early as 1520 the name America began to appear on the maps published for common use. It must be conceded that the crudeness of the inscriptions seems incompatible with what we may well conceive to have been the ceremonious nature of a removal of such importance conducted under royal patronage. But no account whatever of the ceremony has been preserved. We simply know that the removal was permitted by royal order; and the fact that no record of the event is now extant would seem to give plausibility to the conjecture that the remains were transported privately by the family alone. If such was the case, the nature of the inscriptions placed upon the leaden box would depend upon circumstances in regard to which we can now have no knowledge whatever.

In the autumn of 1890 the German explorer Rudolf Cronau determined to investigate this vexed question, and if possible remove it from the domain of doubt. Armed with letters of introduction from the German Government, he passed a month in San Domingo for the purpose of examining every phase of the subject. He not only obtained evidence from the workmen who had exhumed the casket in 1877, but he also secured the privilege of conducting a public examination of the inscriptions. In the presence of the consuls of the United States, England, France, Germany, and Italy, as well as the officials of the cathedral and of the city, he conducted the examination on the 11th of January, 1891. Removing the glass case from the side chapel to the nave of the cathedral, he deposited it upon a table prepared for the purpose. The seals placed upon the case in 1877 having been examined and declared to be intact, the surrounding ribbons were then removed, and with the help of the several keys the case was opened.

It is unnecessary to describe all the processes of investigation. It is, however, important to say that all the inscriptions were photographed upon zinc, in order that they might be etched in exact fac-simile. They have since been reproduced in the first volume of Cronau's "Amerika." As the result of his examination, the author expresses his confident belief that the inscriptions were cut in the sixteenth century; for the processes of oxidation that have taken place since the inscriptions were made, seem to preclude the possibility of their being the work of a modern hand. He states that a careful investigation of all the circumstances attending the opening of the tomb in 1877 failed to give any trace of opportunity for a forging of the inscriptions. The character of the bishop in charge in 1877 was above reproach. The presence of the bullet is, in the opinion of the author, to be regarded as confirmatory proof of genuineness, inasmuch as it is hardly conceivable that it would have been placed in the casket by any fraudulent intent. In short, it is the opinion of Cronau that the difficulties in the way of supporting the theory of fraud are so much greater than those in the way of supporting the theory of genuineness that the charges of fraud must be dismissed, and the theory of genuineness must be finally and conclusively adopted. It seems probable that this conclusion will be accepted by the most judicious investigators of the subject, and that in consequence the belief will come to prevail that the remains of Columbus are now at San Domingo, and not at Havana.

After the ceremony of inspection was completed, the casket and its contents were replaced in the glass box, and this, after being wound about with red, white, and blue ribbons and put under the seals of the several consuls and of the local authorities, was returned to the side chapel as its permanent resting-place.

It would be a great pleasure if we could know that

it is now easy to obtain definite and precise information in regard to those subtile peculiarities of manner and expression which marked and determined the appearance of the Admiral.   But it seems to be impossible.   Of brief descriptions by personal acquaintances there is an abundance ; and in these accounts, moreover, there is substantial agreement.   Trevisan, after meeting the Admiral in 1501, says of him : " He was a robust man, with a tall figure, a ruddy complexion, and a long visage."   Oviedo, who knew him with some intimacy, says : " Of good figure and a stature above the medium, Columbus had strong limbs, keen eyes, a well-proportioned body, very red hair, a complexion that was a little ruddy and marked with freckles."   Las Casas, who saw him often and under diverse circumstances, described him in these words : " He had a figure that was above medium height, a countenance long and imposing, an aquiline nose, clear blue eyes, a light complexion tinged with red, beard and hair blond in youth, but early turned to white.   He was rough in character, with little amiability of speech, affable, however, when he wished to be, and passionate when he was irritated."

In the matter of dress Columbus was in the habit of wearing sombre colors, often appearing in the frock of one of the religious orders.   Las Casas in one place says : " I saw the Admiral at Seville, on his return from the second voyage, clad as a Franciscan friar." Bernaldez relates that he saw him in 1496 " bound about with the cord, of the Franciscan monks;" and Diego Columbus affirms that his father died " clad in the frock of the Franciscan order, to which he was much attached."

It is from these descriptions that the numerous portraits which have passed for likenesses of the Admiral have generally been composed. In all the vast number of paintings and engravings bearing his name, there is probably not one that can be regarded as unquestionably authentic; for it is not known that a single painting or drawing of him was ever made by any person that had ever seen him. Harrisse makes the sweeping statement, "as for the portraits painted, engraved, or sculptured, which figure in the collections, in public places, and in prints, there is not one that is authentic; they are all pure fancy." This learned critic probably means that the numerous pictures have been made, not from life, but from extant descriptions of the Admiral, according to the fancy of the individual artists.

Any one at all familiar with the various portraits that pass, here and there, for likenesses of Columbus, must have been impressed with the fact that, while a few of them present considerable resemblance to one another, they are, almost without exception, lacking in those elements of individuality that are necessary to impress themselves firmly on the attention and memory of the beholder. From the collection as a whole, one is apt to derive a very confused impression as to how Columbus really appeared. If there is to be any exception to this general statement, it should perhaps be made in favour of the portrait by Lorenzo Lotto, recently discovered at Venice. Lotto was quite the most distinguished of the contemporaneous painters whose portraits of Columbus have been preserved. He was absent from Venice during the later years of Columbus's life, and it is possible that he was in Spain during the winter and spring just before the Admiral set out for his fourth voyage. We know that Columbus was in Granada during the winter and spring of 1501–1502, and that during those winter months the Venetian ambassador Pisani and his secretary Camerino were assiduous in courting and entertaining him, in order to obtain maps, charts, and other information about the newly discovered countries. It is possible that Lotto also was present at Granada and that he had an opportunity to paint the portrait from life. But there is no positive evidence on the subject. After all the possibilities are admitted, there is nothing more than a doubtful conjecture that he ever saw the discoverer; still less is it probable that Columbus sat for his portrait.

The painting by Lotto is said by critics to be a striking example in color and in general treatment of this artist's early style. As a portrait, it unquestionably has admirable and striking characteristics; though it is impossible to form any positive opinion as to the accuracy of the likeness. It bears a general resemblance to the picture in the Ministry of the Marine at Madrid, as well as to the Capriolo engraving and to the portrait in the collection of Count D' Orchi at Como. It is scarcely too much to say that Lotto, more than any of the others, seems to have succeeded in delineating certain subtleties of feature and expression which reveal unmistakable character. Whatever the opportunities of this artist for knowing the personal appearance of Columbus, it is certain that he was contemporaneous with the Admiral, and that he lived in an Italian city that was greatly moved by the work of the discoverer. It is known, moreover, that the Venetian ambassador and his secretary were at that time sending home glowing accounts of the significance of the recent voyages. The pre-eminent excellence of the painting, the mood and character which it reveals, and its very striking correspondence with the descriptions of the discoverer by his acquaintances, have led to its selection for the frontispiece of this volume. The portrait was purchased in the summer of 1891 by an enterprising art collector of Chicago.

It remains only to say a concluding word in regard to the estimation in which the character and the work of Columbus are finally to be held.

It is not easy to establish a standard by which to judge of a man whose life was in an age that is past. In defiance of all scholarship, the judgments of critics continue to differ in regard to Alexander, Julius Cæsar, and even Frederick the Great, and Napoleon. On the one hand, nothing can be more unjust than to bring to the judgment of the present age a man whose activities were exerted amid surroundings and influences that have long since changed and passed away; while, on the other, nothing is more unsafe than to regard the opinions of contemporaries as the just and final judgment of humanity.

Between these two dangers we must seek the basis of a judgment in those eternal verities which are applicable to every age. Since civilization began, good men have ever recognized certain principles of right and justice as applicable to all men and all time. Did his life and his work tend to the elevation of mankind? If so, did these results flow from his conscious purpose? If temporary wrong and injustice were done, were these accessory to the firmer establishment of those broad principles which must underlie all security and happiness? These, or such as these, are the questions which it is necessary to ask when we undertake to form a judgment in regard to any man that has performed a great part or exerted a great influence. If we apply these principles in forming an opinion of Columbus, what will be the result?

In point of character, — considering the term in the largest and broadest possible sense,— we shall probably not find very much to admire. The moral atmosphere which he created about him was not much better or much worse than the general atmosphere of the age in which he lived. He entered no protest against any of the abuses of the time. On the contrary, he was ever ready to avail himself of those abuses whenever he could do so to his own advantage. In his age the most sensitive natures were beginning to revolt against the horrors of the slave-trade. But Columbus, in his letters and his journal describing his first voyage, points out the riches that would result to Spain by filling the slave-markets with captives from the newly discovered islands. He repeatedly urged a policy of slave-catching upon the Government; and gave just offence by persistency in such a policy, after receiving a plain intimation that it could not be adopted. There is no evidence that he ever abandoned the idea that a true policy required that ships in going from the mother-country to the islands should be loaded with cattle, and that the same ships in going back from the islands to the mother-country should be loaded with slaves. His first letters glow with accounts of the gentleness and hospitality of the natives. The Indians regarded the new comers as visitors from heaven. When Columbus's own vessel was shipwrecked, the inhabitants on the coast not only rendered every possible assistance, but offered to give up everything they had for the accommodation of the unfortunate visitors. Columbus himself testifies that the native cacique shed " tears of sympathy." Such was the spirit with which the Spaniards were met, and such was the spirit until the policy of kidnapping and devastation was begun. Gradually the Spaniards began to seize the natives as prisoners whenever opportunity offered. Men were found to be less desirable captives than women and children.

Las Casas, the most discriminating and thoughtful, as well as the most humane, of all writers of the time, has in a single sentence described the beginning of the evil. These are his fruitful words: " Since men are never accustomed to fall into a single error, nor into a sin to be committed alone, without a greater one by and by following, so it fell out that the Admiral . . . sent a boat with certain sailors to a house that stood on the side of the river toward the west, and they took and carried off seven women, small and great, with three children. This he says he did because Spaniards with women behave themselves better than without them. A genteel excuse has he given to colour and justify a deed so nefarious." From a general policy, the beginning of which is so significantly described by Las Casas, it came about very naturally that, notwithstanding the noteworthy gentleness of the natives, it was soon discovered that they were not absolutely devoid of the instincts and impulses of human nature. The inevitable result followed. The natives determined to defend their wives and their children. A war of extermination ensued. The number of the inhabitants upon these islands was variously estimated by Las Casas and others of his day. The lowest estimate that can now be reconciled with the original accounts is forty thousand. In the course of the fourteen years between the discovery and Columbus's death the number had been reduced by fully one half; and it was only a few years later when the last of them, hunted like beasts and torn by bloodhounds, perished from the earth. We are accustomed to regard Cortez and Pizarro as exceptional embodiments of inhumanity and cruelty. But Cortez and Pizarro only followed the example that had already been set.

Nor is it possible to acquit Columbus of responsibility for the course that was taken. His position gave him plenary powers. No man ever had fewer scruples in the exercise of all the authority conferred

upon him.   It is indeed true that the policy of the
Spaniards showed itself at its worst after the authority
of Columbus was at an end.   But it is also true that
this policy in all its most deplorable features was in-
augurated by him; and therefore he is to be held
responsible at the bar of history for the evil consequences that ensued.

Nor, again, can we say that the end justified the
means.   Columbus never expected or desired to discover a new country.   His motive in urging the support of the voyages was twofold.   He desired, on the
one hand, to bring back the wealth that would enable
his sovereigns to conquer Jerusalem for Christianity;
and, on the other, to acquire wealth and fame for
himself.   The only condition of success was the finding of vast amounts of gold.   The reports of John de
Mandeville and Marco Polo had filled his mind with
confidence that the necessary gold existed and could
be acquired, if only it could be found.   Hence his
restless activity.   Never dreaming till the day of his
death that the islands he had discovered were not off
the coast of Asia, he thought himself not far away
from the mines that had brought such wealth to Cipango and Cathay.   Everything, therefore, was made
to contribute to this fruitless search.   No thoughtful
person can read the original accounts of the four
voyages without being impressed with the fact that he
was constantly led on from one thing to another by
the alluring reports of gold.   This endless and fruitless quest was the cause of the worst features of his
misgovernment.   The gold mines stubbornly refused

to reveal themselves. Recourse was then had to that pitiless system of *repartimientos,* or enforced labour, which everywhere threw the natives into despair. Then it was that, in the words of Las Casas, "The Admiral went over a great part of the island, making cruel war on all the kings and peoples who would not come into obedience." Elsewhere the same great authority says: "In those days and months the greatest outrages and slaughter of people and depopulation of villages went on, because the Indians put forth all their strength to see if they could drive from their territories a people so murderous and cruel." The original authorities prove beyond question that the policy was simply one of unqualified cupidity, cruelly and relentlessly enforced.

We have already seen that the death of Columbus attracted no general attention and awakened no general comment. This remarkable fact was in strict consonance with the spirit of the time, for the exploits of other voyagers had already caught the public ear and monopolized public attention. Americus Vespucius had returned from his second voyage and had aroused the attention of all Europe by means of his glowing accounts of the new continent. The Cabots from England had at least skirted along the coasts of what is now known as North America. The Portuguese had discovered a safe passage to the Indies by sailing to the south and east, and had begun to raise the question of their rights in consequence of the independent discovery of Brazil, in the year 1500, by Pedro Cabral. Pizarro had learned the art of war under the unscrupulous Ojeda, and Cortez had had the schooling of long interviews with Columbus at San Domingo. Balboa and Magellan had already completed their apprenticeship, and were now about to astonish the world by revealing to it the Pacific Ocean. In the very year of Columbus's death, fishermen from Portugal were already plying their vocation with profit on the banks of Newfoundland ; and less than a year later, the Spaniard Velasco had entered the St. Lawrence. Within the short life of one generation the whole coast from Cape Breton to the Straits of Magellan became the scene of maritime activity. In all parts of the Old World, as well as of the New, it was evident that Columbus had kindled a fire in every mariner's heart. That fire was the harbinger of a new era, for it was not to be extinguished.

INDEX.

MAKERS OF AMERICA.

*The following is a list of the subjects and authors so
far arranged for in this series. The volumes will
be published at the uniform price of $1.00, and
will appear in rapid succession : —*

Peter Stuyvesant (1602–1682), and the Dutch Settlement of New-York. By BAYARD TUCKERMAN, Esq., author of a "Life of General Lafayette," editor of the "Diary of Philip Hone," etc., etc.

Thomas Hooker (1586–1647), Theologian, Founder of the Hartford Colony. By GEORGE L. WALKER, D.D.

Charles Sumner (1811–1874), Statesman. By ANNA L. DAWES.

Thomas Jefferson (1743–1826), Third President of the United States. By JAMES SCHOULER, Esq., author of "A History of the United States under the Constitution."

William White (1748–1836), Chaplain of the Continental Congress, Bishop of Pennsylvania, President of the Convention to organize the Protestant Episcopal Church in America. By Rev. JULIUS H. WARD, with an Introduction by Right Rev. Henry C. Potter, D.D., Bishop of New-York.

Jean Baptiste Lemoine, *sieur* de Bienville (1680–1768), French Governor of Louisiana, Founder of New Orleans. By GRACE KING, author of "Monsieur Motte."

Alexander Hamilton (1757–1804), Statesman, Financier, Secretary of the Treasury. By Prof. WILLIAM G. SUMNER, of Yale University.

Father Juniper Serra (1713–1784), and the Franciscan Missions in California. By JOHN GILMARY SHEA, LL.D.

Cotton Mather (1663–1728), Theologian, Author, Believer in Witchcraft and the Supernatural. By Prof. BARRETT WENDELL, of Harvard University.

Robert Cavelier, *sieur* de La Salle (1643–1687), Explorer of the Northwest and the Mississippi. By EDWARD G. MASON, Esq., President of the Historical Society of Chicago, author of " Illinois " in the Commonwealth Series.

Thomas Nelson (1738–1789), Governor of Virginia, General in the Revolutionary Army. Embracing a Picture of Virginian Colonial Life. By THOMAS NELSON PAGE, author of "Mars Chan," and other popular stories.

George and Cecilius Calvert, Barons Baltimore of Baltimore (1605–1676), and the Founding of the Maryland Colony. By WILLIAM HAND BROWNE, editor of "The Archives of Maryland."

Sir William Johnson (1715–1774), and The Six Nations. By WILLIAM ELLIOT GRIFFIS, D.D., author of "The Mikado's Empire," etc., etc.

Sam. Houston (1793–1862), and the Annexation of Texas. By HENRY BRUCE, Esq.

Joseph Henry, LL.D. (1797–1878), Savant and Natural Philosopher. By FREDERIC H BETTS, Esq.

Ralph Waldo Emerson. By Prof. HERMAN GRIMM, author of "The Life of Michael Angelo," "The Life and Times of Goethe," etc.

DODD, MEAD, & COMPANY,

753 and 755 Broadway, New York.

www.ingramcontent.com/pod-product-compliance
Lightning Source LLC
Chambersburg PA
CBHW031346070726
47496CB00017B/1797